"Ah, Annie, I've never felt this way before. Never needed you so much."

As Mitch rolled her over and pinned her to the bed, coherent thought shattered in the wake of a million sensations. Why? Why had they waited so long to enjoy these exquisite pleasures? They'd wasted so much time, been apart for so long.

"Take it off," Lianne pleaded, bringing his hand to her bra strap. "I don't want anything between us."

With frantic fingers Mitch tore at the satin until she felt the heat from his lips on her bare skin. Her panties followed, shredded with reckless abandon, and his hand slipped lower on her belly. Wanting him naked beside her, Lianne struggled with the zipper on his jeans. With an impatient curse, Mitch got up and stripped them off. Then he stood there for a long moment, looking at her.

"Are you real?" he murmured. "Is it you, or someone I've never touched before?"

Lianne reached out and drew him back onto the bed. "I'm real," she whispered. She placed his palm on her heart. "See?"

"This isn't the way I remember it."

She playfully took a nip at his neck. "That's good, because this time it's going to be *much* better."

Is love sweeter the second time around? That's the question **Kate Hoffmann** decided to answer when she began to write *The Honeymoon Deal*. "I had never written a story featuring a hero and heroine who had once been married to each other, so this gave me a chance to explore a whole new range of emotions," Kate confides. "Finding love after losing it once is a wonderfully romantic notion—and something I hope my readers will enjoy, both on the page and in their own lives."

Fans will want to watch for *Breaking Up Is Hard To Do*, an August 1997 release and Kate's first book for the Love & Laughter series. Write to Kate at: Harlequin Books, 225 Duncan Mill Road, Don Mills, Ontario, Canada, M3B 3K9. She loves to hear from her readers.

Books by Kate Hoffmann

HARLEQUIN TEMPTATION

456—INDECENT EXPOSURE
475—WANTED: WIFE
487—LOVE POTION #9
515—LADY OF THE NIGHT
525—BACHELOR HUSBAND
529—THE STRONG SILENT TYPE
533—A HAPPILY UNMARRIED MAN
546—NEVER LOVE A COWBOY
577—THE PIRATE
599—WICKED WAYS

THE HONEYMOON DEAL
Kate Hoffmann

Harlequin Books

TORONTO • NEW YORK • LONDON
AMSTERDAM • PARIS • SYDNEY • HAMBURG
STOCKHOLM • ATHENS • TOKYO • MILAN
MADRID • WARSAW • BUDAPEST • AUCKLAND

To my editor, Brenda Chin, for her patience, encouragement, and unerring instincts.
This one's for you.

ISBN 0-373-25727-9

THE HONEYMOON DEAL

Copyright © 1997 by Peggy Hoffmann.

Printed in U.S.A.

1

"AND LET US ALL remember that love is indeed a many-splendored thing."

"I wonder if that's what Eunice says when she gets up in the middle of the night and finds that old Mr. Pettigrew has left the toilet seat up again."

"Shh!" Lianne Cooper jabbed Shelly Wilkins in the ribs with her elbow. "She'll hear you." She glanced around the editorial conference room, then looked toward the head of the table, at her boss, Eunice Pettigrew, editor and publisher of *Happily Ever After* magazine.

The white-haired matron was dressed as she always was—in cabbage roses. From the fabric of her dress to the decorations on her shoes, even springing from the ever-present hat perched on her head, cabbage roses of all shapes, sizes and colors seemed to envelop her. If that didn't constitute floral overload, Eunice's office was bedecked with the same fussy flowers, always leaving Lianne craving an elegant stripe or a simple check—or a bottle of aphid killer.

"I thought you said Eunice was going to make an announcement about the new editor for the Honeymoon department," Shelly whispered.

Lianne nodded. "That's what I'd heard. Why else would she call this meeting?"

"To bore us all silly once again with her gooey prattle about love and romance?"

"Shh! She'll hear you!"

The editorial position in the Honeymoon department had been vacant for more than a month, and Lianne suspected that one of the other department editors, from Romance, Life-styles or Weddings, would snatch up the plum position. As an assistant editor, she was the one who would be most affected by Eunice's decision, so she hoped the choice would be someone she liked and respected.

Eunice picked up her reading glasses from where they hung around her neck and peered through them at her notes. "And now I'd like to make an announcement that I'm sure all of you in our *Happily Ever After* family have been waiting for. I've come to a decision regarding our new Honeymoon editor."

"This is it," Lianne said. She held her breath and clutched her fingers in front of her as Eunice cleared her throat and idly rearranged her notes. Suspense just added to the romance of the moment, Lianne suspected, and Eunice was nothing if not a slave to romance.

"Because I believe in rewarding outstanding dedication to our editorial mission, I've chosen an individual who has done more than her share to spread the message of love and commitment to all our readers. A person who is a talented and dependable employee and, more important, a happily married woman. I've decided to promote Lianne Cooper to the position of editor of our Honeymoon department."

The breath rushed from Lianne's lungs and she

blinked hard, certain that she'd misheard the announcement. But when Shelly reached out and gathered her into a hug, she knew there had been no mistake.

Her co-worker patted her on the back. "Why didn't you tell me?" she cried. "Congratulations!"

"Oh, God," Lianne murmured in a tiny voice, completely stunned by the announcement. "What am I going to do?"

Shelly drew back and stared at her with a perplexed frown, but then the rest of Lianne's co-workers gathered around her to offer their own best wishes and Lianne had no time to explain.

There were exclamations of delight and surprise, and a few of thinly veiled envy from the other editors, along with a huge bouquet of roses from Mrs. Pettigrew and a neatly typed memo outlining Lianne's new responsibilities.

For the next ten minutes, Lianne wasn't sure whether she breathed at all. In fact, until she returned to her tiny, windowless office and closed the door behind her, she wasn't even certain that her heart had started beating again. She slowly lowered herself into her desk chair and placed the bouquet of flowers in front of her, the cloying smell irritating her nose.

"Oh, God," she said, this time a little louder. She never thought it would go this far. It had all begun as a little white lie, a little white *necessary* lie, or so she had thought. As she twisted her wedding ring around on her finger, she glanced down at the diamond-studded band and stifled a groan.

A knock sounded on her office door, and Shelly

poked her head inside, a look of concern still etched on her face. "Are you all right?" Her friend slipped inside and closed the door behind her. "You looked a little shell-shocked by Pettigrew's announcement."

"That's an understatement," Lianne replied.

"But this couldn't have come as that much of a surprise. Certainly you must have suspected."

Lianne twisted the ring again. What had ever possessed her to continue wearing it? She'd taken off the large diamond engagement ring, but the wedding band had stayed. "Mrs. Pettigrew didn't mention a word to me," she replied dismally.

A knot twisted in Lianne's stomach as the wedding band inched toward her knuckle. She fought the temptation to yank it off and throw it across the room. She'd worn it more for effect than anything else. She hadn't deliberately meant to deceive, it just seemed...easier. It wasn't a coincidence that everyone who worked at *Happily Ever After* magazine was happily ever *married*. And those who weren't were happily engaged. "I've only worked at the magazine for five years," she said distractedly.

Shelly sat down in a guest chair across from Lianne and stared at her for a long moment. "Hello!" she called, waving her hand in front of Lianne's face. "You don't seem to be very happy about this. A promotion to editor, a big raise, free travel to exotic locations, and you look like someone just offered you a position cleaning toilets at Fenway. Everyone in this office covets the honeymoon job. What's wrong with you?"

A surge of guilt rippled through Lianne and she winced. "I just never expected it. I'm not...not..." She drew in a deep breath. "Qualified." The word rushed out in one big whoosh. She wanted to say "married," but she just couldn't bring herself to admit the truth. She had kept the secret for so long.

Shelly rolled her eyes. "You've been an assistant in the department for three years. You've done all the work that an editor has for half the pay. Of course you're qualified."

"No," Lianne said evenly, "I'm not."

"But you're—"

"Not married," Lianne blurted out. There, that wasn't so bad. Kind of like ripping a Band-Aid off a scraped knee. It only stung for a minute, but now that she'd told the truth, she felt much better. Shelly would know what to do about this dilemma. When it came to office politics, Shelly always knew what to do.

But her friend only laughed. "What are you saying? Of course you're married."

Lianne slowly stood and circled her desk. "No, I'm not."

Reaching past her, Shelly grabbed the small framed picture from Lianne's desk and held it out in front of her. "Then, who is this? It looks an awful lot like you, in a wedding dress. And if I'm not mistaken, that guy in the tux looks like a groom. Look how happy you and—and—what's-his-name are!" She frowned. "What is your husband's name?"

"Mitch," Lianne said, staring at the smiling couple. "And we were happy."

"Were? As in past tense?" Shelly groaned. "Oh, don't tell me you're having marital problems."

"Not unless you consider divorce a problem."

"The guy next to you isn't your husband anymore?"

Lianne took the photo from Shelly's outstretched hands. She'd thought all her dreams had come true—a picture-perfect wedding to her college sweetheart. A bright future as a wife and mother, married to a successful and wealthy attorney, much more than a plumber's daughter from the South End should have ever expected. "He hasn't been for almost five years."

"Does Mrs. Pettigrew know about this?"

"Of course not," Lianne said.

"Oh, hell," Shelly said, leaning back in her chair, her excitement now visibly deflated. "Well, that changes everything. You know how Mrs. Pettigrew feels about marriage and commitment and—" She lowered her voice. "The despicable *D*. She can't even say the word out loud. She considers this magazine her own personal crusade against the one-in-two marriages theory."

"Five minutes after I walked in the front door for my job interview I knew that. It's more than a little obvious."

Her mind flashed back to that day. The first thing she'd noticed were the wedding and honeymoon pictures plastered on every available inch of wall space in the *Happily Ever After* offices. Eunice Pettigrew's office had been even worse. The cabbage roses, more pictures, embroidered pillows with sugary sayings, photos of her husband and family cluttering her desk, and a huge cross-stitch sampler behind her desk with the saying Forever and Ever, Till Death Do Us Part—surrounded, of course, by more cabbage roses. And it hadn't helped that their first topic of conversation had been Lianne's wedding band.

She had hoped for a job with a newspaper or a more prestigious news magazine. But a college degree in journalism didn't count for much when you'd been out of the job market for five years. Even though Lianne knew that her marital status couldn't legally be called into question, she still needed a job, any job, even one as a receptionist at a monthly wedding-and-honeymoon magazine. She'd just walked out on her five-year marriage and she had been desperate—desperate enough to say anything.

To be perfectly honest, she had been married at the time and hadn't yet worked up the nerve to take off her wedding band. The divorce became final six months *after* she got the job. And she'd been happy...sort of. So it wasn't that big a stretch to say she was happily married, was it? At least it didn't seem so at the time.

"I should just tell Mrs. Pettigrew the truth and take my chances," Lianne said.

"Oh, she'll be thrilled," Shelly said cynically. "She'll get that wounded look on her face, and then she'll sigh and sniffle and dab at her eyes with one of her rose-scented embroidered hankies. Then she'll rattle off all sorts of reasons why the world is going to hell in a handbasket because of divorce. And then you'll have to leave, just like your old boss, Cindy, did."

"Cindy left for a job at *Bride's World* magazine."

"After Eunice practically forced her out. I heard that Cindy told Eunice she and her husband were having problems. So Eunice made it her number one priority to fix Cindy's marriage. Cindy got so fed up with Eunice's meddling, she had to leave and find another job. Eunice Pettigrew won't be truly satisfied until everyone in this country is paired off and blissfully happy. I think she was Noah in another lifetime."

"But she can't make a happy marriage a job requirement."

"The Honeymoon editor has always been married. Everyone around here knows that. Besides, Mrs. Pettigrew believes that to write about honeymoons, you have to live them. That's why she pays the editor to get out there and scout destinations, so that you can see what all those newlyweds want out of their honeymoons. She calls it 'keeping in touch with our readers.'"

"I know, but—"

"And scouting honeymoon locations requires a partner, a husband willing to travel, to play the happy honeymooner. A boyfriend or lover sharing your room *simply won't do.*" Shelly finished in a perfect imitation of Eunice's tone.

"I don't have a husband. Or a lover or even a boyfriend, for that matter. So what's the use?"

"What's the use? You've got the best job in the place. If I could write worth a damn, I'd go after it. And our Honeymoon editors have all gone on to bigger and better jobs."

"But I don't have a husband," Lianne repeated.

Shelly waved her hand dismissively. "Do you want the job?"

"I'd love the job," she admitted. "The salary is twice what I'm making. And with my dad's illness, he and my mom have been scraping just to get by. I would love to give them a little extra so they could enjoy their retirement."

"If you really want the job, you'll just have to find yourself a husband for a few weeks each year. You're an attractive woman—it shouldn't be too hard. It's not like Eunice is going to be there in the room with you."

Lianne shook her head. "But I don't want a husband. I had one and I didn't like it at all."

"Aren't you listening?" Shelly asked. "Just find a guy to pretend he's your husband. Eunice would never need to know that you're not blissfully wed. Personally, my husband would jump at four free vacations a year."

"Then you'd be willing to lend him to me?" Lianne asked.

"Not a chance," Shelly said. "I've grown rather fond of the slob. Besides, I want to keep my job. It took me seven years and countless sappy stories about my loving spouse before Eunice promoted me. I'm head of circulation and I'm very happily married, even though we still haven't resolved our own toilet seat issues yet. Find yourself your own husband."

Lianne rubbed her temples. "Why are we even talking about this? I'm going to have to tell her the truth. Or maybe I should just refuse the promotion."

"Don't you dare!"

"What else can I do?"

"Was the divorce very nasty?"

Lianne shook her head. "No, it was quite amicable. We grew apart. Or maybe we just never grew together."

"Then, why don't you just call up Mitch?"

"But Mitch and I haven't talked to each other in over three years, and we haven't seen each other since the divorce became final. I can't call him up out of the blue. What am I supposed to say? 'Hi, Mitch, this is your ex-wife. Could you clear your schedule so you can pretend to be my husband for a few weeks?' He wouldn't do that much when we were married."

"What do you have to lose?" Shelly asked. "I mean, besides the promotion." She snatched up the phone and held it out to Lianne. "Come on, give it a try. The guy must still owe you a few favors, doesn't he?"

Mitch had always been generous when it came to his wife. Lianne had suspected that throwing money her way had been the only way he could justify ignoring her as he had. It had come as a total surprise to him when Lianne informed him that she wasn't interested in his money. All she asked for was a marriage and the time together to nurture it. When he couldn't give her that, she asked for a divorce instead.

"Mitch is a very busy man," Lianne said. "He's a partner in his family's law firm. Cooper, Cooper and Cooper."

Shelly gasped, her eyes growing wide. "He's one of the Cutthroat Coopers?" she asked. "They're one of Boston's oldest law firms. They represent some of New England's biggest corporations. You were married to a Cooper?"

Lianne nodded. "The third Cooper on the masthead."

"Let me get this straight. You were married to a Cooper and you're living in a one-bedroom apartment and driving a thirty-year-old car. Who was your divorce attorney, Bozo the Clown?"

"The Mustang is a classic. I lost my virginity in that car. And I didn't want anything from Mitch or his family. I never fit in on the south slope of Beacon Hill. My blood wasn't blue enough. So I settled for the dog and the car and just enough money to tide me over until I could get on my feet."

"That's all?" Shelly shook her head. "Yeah, I'd say the guy owes you. He owes you big time. What's his number? I'll talk to him myself."

Lianne grabbed the phone out of her friend's hand. "No, you won't."

"Then dial," Shelly ordered. "If this creep can't give you seven days of his precious time a couple of times a year, then I'm sure he won't mind you renegotiating the divorce agreement."

"I'm not going to do that," Lianne said.

"Well, he doesn't have to know that, does he. Dial."

Reluctantly, Lianne took the phone and slowly dialed Mitch's office number, a number that came back to her with startling clarity.

An unfamiliar voice answered the phone. "Cooper, Cooper and Cooper Law Offices."

Lianne's grip tightened on the handset. "Mitchell Cooper, please," she said, the tremor in her voice making it nearly impossible to speak.

"Senior, junior or the third?" the receptionist asked efficiently.

"The—the third."

The receptionist paused. "I'm afraid Mr. Cooper isn't in. May I take a message?"

Lianne bit back a frustrated sigh. Why did this have to be so difficult? "Do you know when he'll be back? It's very important that I reach him."

"I'm sorry, but I don't have that information. Perhaps someone else might be able to help you. May I ask who's calling?"

"This is his wife. I mean, his ex-wife, Lianne." She glanced up at Shelly and her friend gave her an encouraging smile.

This time the receptionist paused for more than just a moment. "I'm sorry. I didn't realize Mr. Cooper had been married. One moment, please."

Music replaced the woman on the other end of the line, and Lianne fought the urge to hang up then and there. "He's not in," she muttered.

"Where is he?" Shelly asked.

"I don't know. Maybe in court."

"When will he be back?"

Lianne shot Shelly an irritated look and held out the phone. "Would you like to talk to her?"

"Mrs. Cooper?"

Lianne slapped the phone back to her ear and cleared her throat. "Yes?"

"I just spoke with Mr. Cooper, Senior, and he wanted me to let you know that Mr. Cooper the Third no longer works here. He took a leave of absence last year."

Lianne frowned. "A leave of absence?" Why would Mitch take a leave of absence? The man lived and breathed Cooper, Cooper and Cooper. He'd once said they'd have to carry him out the twin mahogany doors in a coffin. "Is he all right?"

The receptionist lowered her voice. "I don't know the specifics, but I believe Mr. Cooper, Senior, mentioned a medical problem. A...serious illness."

Lianne's throat tightened. "I—I'll call him at home."

"I believe he recently moved to an apartment near Boston University," the receptionist added helpfully.

"Can you give me his new address and phone number?"

"I have an address but I don't think he has a phone. One moment, please."

Lianne picked up a pencil and nervously tapped it on the desk as she waited, her mind jumbled with concern. A medical problem. And he'd moved out of their comfortable Beacon Hill town house—the place she'd spent five years turning into the perfect home. The town house just three blocks away from her in-laws, the only proper place for a partner at Cooper, Cooper and Cooper to live.

She'd tried so hard to be the perfect wife—the decorating, the gourmet cooking, the volunteer work with the most prominent charities. She had hoped to slip into life with the Boston Brahmins as if she'd been born into it. But that had never happened. No matter how hard she tried to fit in, she had always been an outsider.

After the divorce, she'd realized that nothing would have brought her acceptance. She just hadn't been brought up to deal with the unspoken expectations—to stand in the background while her husband spent all his time and energy making money.

So she left Mitch and the elegant town house and found a tiny flat back on the South End, taking only Ir-

ving the Drooling Dog and a car in the divorce settle-
ment. She went out in search of a new life and she'd
found one. Except for her mistaken marital status at the
magazine, everything had turned out pretty well.

She grimaced. But what had happened with Mitch.
To be the third Cooper on the Cooper, Cooper and
Cooper letterhead had been his only goal in life, to the
exclusion of everything else. Every possibility that
came to Lianne's mind was something she didn't want
to consider.

The receptionist came back on the line and Lianne
scribbled the address on a scrap of paper. Thanking the
receptionist, she hung the phone up.

"Well?" Shelly asked.

Lianne stared at the address for a long time. "He
doesn't work for the firm anymore. He took a leave of
absence." She took a deep breath. "Something's
wrong." Slowly, she stood and grabbed her purse from
the top drawer of her desk. "I've got to go," she murmured.

"Where?"

"Where else?" Lianne said as she hurried to the
door. "To see Mitch."

"Then, you're going to ask him to be your husband
for a week?"

"No. I'm going to find out what's wrong. You don't
know Mitch Cooper. There's only one reason he'd
leave his job at Cooper, Cooper and Cooper."

"And what's that?" Shelly asked.

"He's ill." Lianne covered her lips with her fingers
and stifled a cry of alarm. "For all I know, he could be
dying. I've got to see him."

MITCH POKED IMPATIENTLY at the half-frozen TV dinner, then rummaged through the garbage to retrieve the box. Thirty-five minutes at 350 degrees. So at 550 degrees, fifteen minutes should have been sufficient if he'd done the math correctly. Actually, 700 degrees would have been best, but his oven didn't go that high.

He scanned the directions again, pondered the importance of preheating the oven, then grabbed the dinner and a fork and dug in.

He'd just discovered the miracle of frozen dinners the other night at the grocery store and had bought a freezer full. Until then, the freezer aisle had been of interest only for its selection in the ice cream case. But he'd been on a search for French fries, and when he stumbled across the Hungry-Man dinners, they had seemed like a gift from the gods, a product made for the divorced man with a limited food budget and rudimentary culinary skills.

He'd never had to worry about his own nutrition until a few months ago. The whole time he'd been in college and law school, the Cooper family cook had kept him well fed in-between classes, studying and clerking at the family firm. He'd married Lianne right after law school, and she had taken over where the cook had left off. After the divorce, he'd eaten out nearly every night, and when he hadn't, he'd ordered takeout.

But that had all ended the day he walked out the doors of Cooper, Cooper and Cooper. The day he'd walked away from his partnership, his career and his six-figure salary. And his father…most of all, his father.

It still troubled him to think about that day, about the argument that had precipitated his decision to leave. But he'd had enough—enough of the pressure and the maneuvering and the need to win at all costs. He'd thought the firm would be his life as it had been for his grandfather and his father. But in the five years since his divorce, he'd come to realize what Lianne had long before. Mitch Cooper was not a man he particularly liked.

He'd asked for a simple leave of absence, time to regroup and decide what he wanted to do. But his father had refused, and what had started as a request for a short sabbatical had turned into a full-scale battle, ending only when Mitch scribbled a letter of resignation on a yellow legal pad and threw it at his father. He'd heard that office gossip had him recovering from a nagging virus. But he'd been gone for almost a year now. Sooner or later his father was going to have to admit that his son wasn't suffering from anything more than a bad case of self-disgust.

He hadn't owned any equity in the firm so he took nothing with him but his briefcase. He'd even left his diplomas on the wall behind his desk.

It only took a few months to realize that he could no longer afford dinners out, the expensive car he leased or the rent on the Beacon Hill town house. So he bought a bicycle, found a cheaper place to live and took a job as an instructor at Boston University's law school. And for the first time in as long as he could remember, he truly enjoyed getting up in the morning. There were no phones, no stress, just quiet and contentment. Hell, he was even beginning to enjoy cooking for himself.

He glanced back down at his dinner. With his knife,

he methodically mixed the half-frozen meat loaf with the burnt gravy and was about to taste the results of his efforts when his security buzzer rang. He stepped away from the stove and wove his way through the boxes of books in the living room, then punched the security button.

"Yeah?" he shouted, irritated that his dinner had been interrupted. "Who is it?"

"Mitch?"

An angry retort died in his throat. He shook his head, certain that he'd been mistaken. The person waiting downstairs couldn't be Lianne. He hadn't spoken to his ex-wife in...what? Three years. Hadn't seen her in five. What would she be doing here now?

Warily, he reached out and pushed the button. "Yeah, this is Mitch Cooper. Who are you?"

There was a long pause on the other end. "Mitch, it's Lianne."

He stared at the intercom. "Lianne?"

"Your ex-wife. Lianne." He heard her clear her throat. "Cooper," she added, as if her identity needed clarification. "Remember?"

Mitch smiled to himself. "I remember who you are, Annie. I'm just surprised to hear your voice. What are you doing here?"

"Can—can I come up?"

"I'll be right down," he said. He grabbed a faded T-shirt from a pile of clean laundry on the floor and tugged it over his head, then took the steps from his third-floor flat two at a time. Through the beveled glass window of the front door, he saw her standing on the porch, staring out at the street.

He stared at her, his hand resting on the doorknob. She had changed since he'd last set eyes on her. Her hair was different, loose and casual and a few shades darker than the blond in their wedding picture. He pushed the door open and she spun around at the sound.

"Hi," he said, suddenly unable to think of a snappy greeting.

She smiled hesitantly, and he found his gaze instantly captivated by her face. He'd always thought she was pretty enough, but he hadn't remembered how beautiful she really was. How could he have forgotten something that, in just seconds, had already imprinted itself in his mind? "How did you know where to find me?" he asked.

"I called your office." She studied him openly, her gaze flitting from his face to his feet and back up again. "They told me you had taken a leave."

"I'm surprised they gave you any information at all. These days I'm pretty much *persona non grata* at Cooper, Cooper and Cooper. I expect my name will come off the door and the stationery before too long."

A shocked expression suffused her features. "How can you say that?" she cried. "They'd never be so cruel. It's not your fault you had to leave. You'll be back, you just need some time." She paused, then scanned the peeling paint on the ramshackle porch. "Why did you move out of the town house?"

"I'm not working at Cooper anymore. I couldn't afford it," Mitch replied.

"Certainly your father could have helped you out."

Mitch's jaw tensed. "I don't need any help from my father," he replied in an even voice.

"What about your trust fund?"

"That's not available anymore." He drew in a deep breath, ready to change the subject. "So how are you? How is Irving?"

"I'm fine. The dog is fine."

"Still have that drooling problem?" Mitch asked.

Lianne smiled. "I slipped on the problem just this morning."

Mitch laughed out loud. She shifted nervously, then forced a short laugh of her own before drawing in a deep breath. He could see her groping for words, clearly uneasy in his presence.

"So how are you feeling? Are—are you all right?"

He shrugged, baffled by the concern in her wide green eyes. "I haven't been eating very well, but other than that, I'm doing okay."

She took a step closer. "You look a little thin," she said. "And a little pale. Have you had something to eat today?"

Mitch stared at his ex-wife. They hadn't seen each other for five years and all she could talk about was his eating habits? Certainly there were other things they could discuss—like what the hell she was doing standing on his doorstep. Like why she looked so beautiful to him, and why he was having to fight like hell to keep his hands off her.

"I—I could make you something to eat," she offered. "Would you like me to do that?"

"Sure," Mitch said, trying to hide his confusion. "I could eat." He pushed open the door and followed her inside. "I'm on the third floor. There are times when I'd kill for an elevator."

"I can imagine," she said softly, looking over her shoulder. "It can't be good for you to climb all these stairs."

He followed her up the stairs, deliberately staying a few steps behind to enjoy the view of her backside. He'd remembered her as thinner, with an almost girlish figure. But somewhere along the way, she'd grown a few very womanly curves. And they'd cropped up in all the right places.

When they came to his landing, he reached out to open the door for her. "It's a little messy. I've lived here for five months but still haven't worked up the energy to unpack."

She made a quick survey of the apartment while he scrambled to pick up some of the dirty clothes tossed across the furniture.

"It's very...roomy," she said. She glanced out the big bay window. "And you can almost see the river from here."

"Kitchen's in back." He frantically stuffed a pair of jeans and a pile of socks under the sofa cushion, then followed her. Bracing his shoulder on the kitchen door-jamb, he watched as she searched through the cupboards and the refrigerator.

"I tried to make one of those TV dinners," he said, pointing to the disaster on the stove, "but the oven must be broken."

She stood in front of the freezer. "This is all you have? Frozen dinners and ice cream? You'll have to start eating better." She pulled one out and tore open the end of the box. "I'll put this in the microwave and it will be ready in a few minutes."

"I wouldn't do that. I tried last night and the thing almost exploded."

"You can't put TV dinners in the microwave unless you take them out of the foil plate."

Mitch raised an eyebrow at the revelation, then memorized her actions as she put the contents of the tray on a plate. "They should put those rules on the box," he said.

Lianne glanced over her shoulder again and graced him with a smile—a smile that sent a flood of warmth through his blood. "They do. But then, you were never one to read directions, were you? Why don't you go sit down and I'll bring you your dinner when it's ready."

Mitch strolled back into the living room. A little soft music might be in order. He picked out a compact disc and flipped on the expensive stereo system they'd purchased after their wedding. The sounds of soft jazz flowed out of the speakers, and his mind flashed back to the night they'd first set up the stereo at the town house. They'd just moved in after a weeklong honeymoon in Bermuda, and they'd eaten takeout Chinese while they listened to a Miles Davis album.

Their marriage had been good—once. Or had it? He'd spent so little time with her during those five years that he wasn't quite sure if she had ever shared that favorable opinion. She must have loved him or she wouldn't have married him. But somewhere along the way, she'd stopped. And he was pretty certain it had been his fault.

Marriage had always been part of the logical progression of his life, expected by his family. First college, then law school, a job with the firm and then a partnership. His professional life had been mapped out from the time he was born. And his personal life had been just as rigidly planned. The only deviation had been falling in love with a girl from a family of "limited means," as his mother had disdainfully said.

And then the divorce. That had been a major deviation, and a disappointment to the family. They'd all expected him to quickly find a replacement for Lianne—from a more suitable family, of course—and remarry, to put his personal life back on track in time to provide a Mitchell Cooper the Fourth before the Third turned thirty. But there had been no replacement for Lianne.

A few minutes later, she reappeared, carrying the plate and a fork. He sat down on the sofa, and she placed the meal on the coffee table in front of him, then crossed her arms clumsily.

"Aren't you going to eat?" he asked, trying to catch her gaze.

She shook her head, then turned and walked to the bay window. "I'm not very hungry," she replied, almost as an afterthought.

He watched her for a long moment, wondering at the woman standing in the soft afternoon light. Who was she? He'd been married to her for five years, yet he'd never been able to get inside her head. After five years, she seemed an odd contradiction, as unknown as a stranger, yet familiar as a lover.

He pushed off the couch and crossed the room. Placing his hands on her shoulders, he turned her around to face him.

He'd meant only to look into her eyes, to try once again to read what was there. But the moment he touched her, an overwhelming urge took hold of him and he bent his head and brushed his mouth against hers, lingering. He'd only wanted to see if she tasted as sweet as he remembered, but once he started, he couldn't seem to stop. His tongue traced along her lips, probing gently. Her mouth melted beneath his and he deepened his kiss.

As he reluctantly drew back, her eyes widened. She held her breath, then swallowed hard and blinked, as if trying to shake herself from a dream. "Wha-what was that for?"

Mitch let his hands slide off her shoulders, then ran one through his hair. Good question, he thought to himself. Right now, he didn't have an answer. "I guess I felt like kissing you," he murmured. "It's been a long time."

Her gaze fixed on a spot somewhere beyond his left shoulder. "Something to drink," she murmured, before stepping around him. "You need something to drink."

With that she hurried from the room, leaving Mitch to wonder if his kiss had had the same startling effect on her as it had on him.

LIANNE BRACED HER HANDS on the edge of the counter and drew a long, steadying breath. Her heart still thumped erratically in her chest, and she felt a little breathless. And inside her head, his kiss replayed itself over and over again, like a skipping record, each time causing the sensations to come flooding back.

She touched her bottom lip, then rubbed at it, hoping to wipe away the heat of his mouth. She'd kissed him countless times when they'd been married, but his kisses had never affected her quite this way.

Perhaps it was because he seemed nothing at all like the man she'd married. His once well-trimmed dark hair now brushed his collar, shaggy and unkempt, giving him a slightly disreputable look. And the jeans that hugged his long legs were faded and thin at the knees. The Mitch Cooper she remembered used to throw his jeans out once they began to fade—and he'd never have been seen in public in a T-shirt.

He'd been a suit-and-tie kind of guy, buttoned-down and conservative, a guy whose idea of danger amounted to leasing a red car. But the man who kissed her just moments ago was definitely dangerous, in a disturbing and surprising way.

"Are you planning to spend the rest of your visit hiding in my kitchen?"

Lianne spun around to find Mitch standing in the doorway. He held his plate in front of him as he methodically devoured his meat loaf dinner, while still keeping his eyes fixed on her.

"Wha-what would you like to drink?" she asked.

"I think my choices in this kitchen are limited to water and drain cleaner. Water would be fine."

Lianne fumbled through the cupboards until she found a plastic Celtics cup, then filled it from the kitchen faucet. She held it out to him. "It's good to drink a lot of fluids when you're sick," she murmured.

"Sick?"

"Can you tell me what you have?"

He stepped closer and placed his plate on the counter. "You mean besides an overwhelming urge to kiss you again?"

She nodded, staring down at the congealed gravy and mushy carrots.

"It tastes like meat loaf," he said.

She sighed in frustration, then looked up to meet his gaze. His blue eyes seemed uncomfortably close. "I mean, what do the doctors say?"

"What doctors?"

"You haven't seen a doctor?"

"Why would I need a doctor?"

"Because you're ill," Lianne said.

A slow smile curved his lips and he chuckled, a deep, warm sound that started in his chest and gave her the shivers. "Oh, you talked to my father. What story has he been circulating this week?"

"You're not sick?"

"Is that why you came here?" Mitch shook his head. "Annie, I left the firm because I was sick of facing Mitchell Cooper the Third every morning in the mirror. I was sick of working sixteen-hour days defending clients whose positions were indefensible."

She felt the color rise in her cheeks. "But I—I thought you had some disease. I thought you were—"

"Dying?" Mitch chuckled.

"Well, what was I supposed to think? You left the firm. You said they'd have to carry you out in a coffin."

"At first my father told everyone I was on vacation. He was certain I'd be back after a week. When it stretched to three, he informed my secretary that I was on safari in Africa and couldn't get to a phone. After a month, he told them I'd picked up a virus in Africa that I couldn't shake. I have no idea what he's telling my clients now, and frankly, I don't care." He reached out and cupped her cheek in his palm. "Hey, it's nice to know that you still care, but I'm healthy. A little underfed, but feeling great."

She clenched her jaw beneath his touch as her temper rose. "How could you let me think you were dying?"

"Don't blame me. I had no idea what was going on in that head of yours."

"You took advantage!" She pushed his hand away. "Oh, that's just like a Cooper. Find a weakness and press the advantage. You knew I was feeling sorry for you and you kissed me."

"You kissed me back," he said.

She gasped. "I did not! I was only trying to be nice."

"That was not a *nice* kiss, Lianne."

"No, it wasn't," she snapped. "It was a pity kiss and nothing more."

"Come on, Annie, we were married for five years. I can read you a little better than that."

"Oh, really? Well, read this." Lianne grabbed his plate of food from the counter and slammed it into his chest. Then she turned on her heel and headed toward the door.

"Annie, wait!"

"Wait? For what? For you to make a complete fool of me all over again?"

"I'm sorry," Mitch called. "I wasn't trying to make you feel foolish. Come on, let me make it up to you.

Stay for a little while longer. We haven't talked in years. You can't just walk out like this."

She stopped, her hand on the doorknob. She didn't want dinner. She didn't want him to kiss her. She didn't want to talk to him. In fact, she didn't want anything from him except—

Except...

Slowly, she took her hand off the doorknob and turned to him. He wanted to make it up to her? Well, she knew the perfect way. "All right," she said. "I'll give you a chance to make it up to me."

"Anything," Mitch said, wiping the gravy from his T-shirt. "I'll take you out to dinner. Something better than—" he shook a glob of mashed potato from his fingers and it landed with a plop on the hardwood floor "—meat loaf."

"I have a much better idea," Lianne said.

"What?" Mitch asked. "Tell me."

"There is something you could do for me. Something that would mean a lot. Something that would completely make up for your boorish behavior."

"Name it," Mitch said.

Lianne straightened and crossed her arms over her chest. "I want you to be my husband for a week."

2

THE WORDS WERE BARELY out of her mouth before she wanted to take them back. He'd given her the perfect opening and she'd taken it. But now the lunacy of her request hung in the air between them.

"I've got to go," she said. She yanked the door open and hurried out.

"Lianne, wait!"

She took the stairs as fast as she could, but Mitch was right on her heels, catching up with her on the front porch. He reached out and grabbed her arm, but she wriggled out of his grasp. "Let me go!"

"Not a chance," Mitch said, this time holding tight. He pulled her toward the front steps. "Sit," he ordered.

Reluctantly, Lianne did as she was told, then watched him pace back and forth at the bottom of the porch steps. She cursed silently. She should have known he wouldn't let her go without a complete explanation. Why hadn't she left when she had the chance, *before* she'd made a complete idiot of herself?

"Would you like to say that again?" Mitch asked. "I'm not sure I heard you right."

"You did," she said stubbornly. She tried to stand up, but he gently pushed her back down. "Just forget it. I didn't mean it, I was—"

"No, I don't think I want to forget this, Annie." He rubbed the back of his neck. "Perhaps an explanation might be in order. First, you show up on my porch, thinking I have some fatal illness. You make me dinner and we share what you politely term a 'pity kiss.' Then I ask if there's anything I can do for you and you ask me to marry you for a week. Somehow, I get the feeling that you didn't really come here to inquire about my health."

"I did so. And I never said a word about marriage," Lianne grumbled, hugging her knees to her chest. "I wanted you to *pretend* to be my husband. Just for a week. It's all very simple." She paused. "At least Shelly made it sound that way at first."

"I can't wait to hear this. Why don't we begin with Shelly."

For the next ten minutes, Lianne felt as if she were involved in an intense cross-examination. And Mitch would settle for nothing but the truth. He fired questions at her and she answered, trying to make her hare-brained idea for keeping her new job sound as logical and practical as possible, and attempting to shift the entire blame for the concept onto her co-conspirator, Shelly Wilkins. But no matter what she said, Mitch was not satisfied.

"You know that this Mrs. Pettigrew cannot consider marital status as a condition of employment," he said. "It's against the law."

Lianne nodded.

"So, the way I see it, you don't need a husband. You need a good lawyer. We'll just bring a lawsuit."

"No!" Lianne jumped up from her place.

"Annie, this is so cut-and-dried, a law clerk could settle it. You've got a solid case. Hell, I'll represent you."

"I don't want a lawsuit. I want this job. I've only been at the magazine for five years, and Mrs. Pettigrew has shown a great deal of confidence in me to promote me so soon."

"There are other jobs," Mitch said. "The publisher of *Boston Magazine* is one of my clients. One of my former clients," he corrected himself. "I could get you an interview there in a—"

"I don't want your help," Lianne insisted. "I got this job on my own, and I got this promotion on my own. This is a chance for me to prove myself. And to pay back a little of the money my parents spent on my college education. I don't want to mess it up. Now, either you're going to help me or you're not."

Mitch shook his head. "As your lawyer, I have to advise you that you—"

"You're not my lawyer!"

"And I'm not your husband, either. Not anymore."

She plopped back down on the top step and braced her chin in her hand, pouting. "Well, maybe you could act like a friend and understand what this means to me."

He raked his hands through his hair and sighed.

"I could make it worth your while," she offered, gazing up at him.

Mitch's right eyebrow shot up, and he gave her a look that she **was c**ertain had withered more than one witness on the stand. "Would that be monetary compensation we're discussing? Or just hot sex?" he asked.

She flushed first, then shot him an exasperated glare. He was taking such pleasure in embarrassing her that her fierce look made no impression. "I'm prepared to offer you something I think you'll find quite appealing."

Mitch grinned. "That would be the hot sex, then."

"A free weeklong vacation to a wonderful resort in the Poconos. All meals and drinks are paid for. So is transportation. We'll have a luxurious cabin in the mountains."

Mitch stopped his pacing and hooked his thumbs in the pockets of his jeans. "Now you have my interest. I assume we'll be sharing a bed?"

"You'll be sleeping on the floor," Lianne said.

He shook his head. "I don't think so."

She ground her teeth. "All right, I'll sleep on the floor."

Mitch waited, and when she didn't continue, he slowly shook his head. "Is that your best offer? Surely you don't expect me to consider such inadequate compensation for exploiting my integrity. You've asked me to misrepresent myself, and for this I get a bed and a few free meals?"

She ground her teeth. "All right. You can have Irving every other weekend for a year," she said.

"That's a start," he said. "But I was thinking more along the lines of transportation."

"I told you, our transportation would be paid for. We'll fly into—"

"*My* transportation," he emphasized. "I want my Mustang back."

Lianne gasped. "My car? You want me to give you my car?"

He shrugged. "I've always thought of it as *my* car since it was a graduation gift from my parents. Besides, Boston has a wonderful subway system. I'm sure you could make do. And with this new salary of yours, you could buy yourself a new car."

He was right. With this new job, she could easily afford a car payment, and much more. And she took the subway to work every day, anyway. The Mustang usually sat in the parking lot of her apartment building all day long. She could do without the Mustang if it meant saving her career and giving a little something back to her folks.

She groaned inwardly. What choice did she have? Mitch for the Mustang. "All right. The car in return for *four* weeks of my choosing."

"Four weeks now? I teach a class two nights a week at Boston University Law School. What if I can't find someone to cover for me?"

"That's your problem," Lianne said. "Besides, it's a classic car, and it's worth more than a week of your time."

"All right. Four weeks for the Mustang. And I take ownership after the first week. And joint custody of Irving. Every other weekend and alternate holidays."

"How did Irving get back into the deal?"

"You never officially took him off the table," Mitch said.

Resigned that he would get the better of her no matter what she said, Lianne pushed herself up from the step and held out her hand. "All right, it's a deal."

But he merely shoved his hands deeper into his jeans pockets. He studied her openly, his blue eyes discerning every shift in her expression. "I'll consider your offer and get back to you."

"Hey, what is that supposed to mean? We have a deal."

Mitch slowly climbed the steps until he stood beside her. "It means exactly what I said. I'll get back to you." He took her chin in his hand and bent his head toward her, but at the last minute, he changed course and gave her a chaste kiss on the cheek.

"When? I have to know. Now!"

He smiled, a sexy, teasing smile that made her want to scream and pull her hair out. The man she'd remembered as so stoic and serious, so...dull, had turned into a profligate tease, a quality that had a very disconcerting effect on her.

"Soon enough," he said.

He pushed the front door open and gave her one last look, then disappeared. She stood on the porch for a long time, staring at the closed door and feeling as if she'd just been thoroughly bamboozled.

"My only car and my drooling dog in exchange for a temporary husband," she muttered. "A husband I had the good sense to dump years ago." She sighed. "I should have my head examined."

Lianne turned and jogged down the front steps. But as she glanced back over her shoulder at Mitch's building, she had to wonder whether the man she'd just struck a deal with was anything like the man she'd married ten years ago. That Mitch Cooper had been a dependable and honorable man—at least that's how she remembered him.

But *this* Mitchell Cooper seemed more like the devil in disguise.

LIANNE STARED AT HER computer screen, her gaze focused on the twelve-month editorial plan she'd just completed. It wasn't bad for an editor with only two days' experience. Yesterday, she contacted all eleven of her freelance travel writers, soliciting their ideas and adding some of her own, until she'd achieved the perfect balance of honeymoon destinations, spread cleverly over the next year's monthly issues.

Mrs. Pettigrew would be impressed, she mused. How could she not be? Eunice would study the plan and instantly see that she had chosen the best possible candidate to be the editor of the Honeymoon department...married or not.

Lianne leaned back in her chair and braced her hands on the arms. Perhaps that was all she needed to do. Excel at her job, make such a smashing success of the Honeymoon department that Mrs. Pettigrew wouldn't be bothered in the least by her marital status.

"Dream on," she murmured to herself.

It wasn't as if she had a choice anymore. In the two days since she'd seen Mitch, she'd waited for his call, jumping every time the phone rang. He'd obviously decided against getting involved in her scheme.

Could she blame him? If he'd come to her with an identical request, she would have flatly refused. They were divorced, after all, and for good reason. One didn't spend a week sharing a luxurious mountain cabin with one's ex-husband and not expect a certain amount of...hanky-panky. A smile quirked the corners of her mouth. Or hot sex, as Mitch had termed it.

They'd always shared a decent sex life, although she'd had nothing to compare it to at the time. Mitch had been her first—and she'd thought her last—lover. There had been a few others since the divorce, but she'd come to the realization that although sex could be an enjoyable evening's entertainment, it didn't necessarily make the earth move or the angels sing.

Sex had always been so...restrained between them, although that had probably been more her fault than his. They'd shared nothing close to what the articles in the Romance section of the magazine suggested. Sensual massage, a bath for two by candlelight, a sexy striptease. She stifled a moan. At the time, she would have been mortified to suggest anything of the sort to Mitch.

But now...

A clumsy knock sounded at her open office door, and she turned to find Shelly standing in the hallway. Her co-worker's gaze was fixed somewhere down the corridor, and she waved her hand frantically. "I think you'd better get out here," she called.

Lianne frowned. "What is it?"

Shelly turned to her, shooting her an impatient grimace. "Your *husband* is here."

"But I don't have—"

"Your husband is *here*," Shelly repeated. "He's in the lobby chatting up Mrs. Pettigrew."

"Mitch?" Lianne jumped out of her chair and raced to the door. "Mitch is here?"

"God, is he gorgeous," Shelly said, her voice breathless, her hand patting her chest. "Why didn't you tell me he was such a doll? And so charming. For a husband like that, I'd collect his dirty socks with my teeth."

Lianne clutched her hands in front of her and risked a quick peek down the hall. "Why is he here?"

Shelly grabbed her arm and pulled her out the door. "How should I know? He's your husband. Go find out."

"Ex-husband," Lianne clarified.

"Well, that's not what he told Mrs. Pettigrew. In fact, he's got her completely snowed. He's letting her in on all sorts of personal things about you two. If I were you, I'd get out there and see what he wants. Before he slips up."

Lianne smoothed her skirt and straightened her jacket, then took a deep breath and headed down the hallway. She found Mitch exactly where Shelly had said he'd be, deep in conversation with Mrs. Pettigrew.

The older woman caught sight of her as she approached and held out her hand. "Here's your Lianne!" she cried.

Lianne winced inwardly. Mitch's Lianne. Just the sound of it grated on her nerves. As if he had total control over her life. Her jaw tightened and she bit back a curse. He didn't control her life, but she'd opened the door for him to control her professional future. What was he doing here?

"Dear, I was just making the acquaintance of your husband," Eunice cooed. "I was telling him how we feel these regular honeymoon trips for our editor are very important." She turned back to Mitch. "They help us keep our fingers on the pulse of today's newly-weds." She patted Mitch on the arm, then turned back to Lianne. "He's doing us a great favor by accompanying you, so you might get a real feel for the honeymoon atmosphere. In fact, he says he can't wait to get to the Poconos."

Lianne tried hard not to appear startled. Her gaze shifted to "her" Mitch and he gave her a conspiratorial wink. Relief flooded through her. So he'd made up his mind. He had decided to help her. "Yes," she said, her voice a bit shaky. "Mitch has always been fond of travel."

Eunice frowned and looked back and forth between the two of them. "That's odd. Mitch was just telling me that he hasn't had a vacation since your honeymoon."

"I've always *wanted* to travel," Mitch said smoothly. "I've just never had the time. But this is a perfect opportunity. Isn't it, *darling?*"

Lianne sent him what she hoped was a warning glare, unable to ignore his emphasis on the endearment. "A perfect opportunity," she repeated softly. And if she managed to extract them both from Eunice's prying nature, she'd take the opportunity to wipe that smug grin off his face. He was having fun with this, making her squirm, watching her teeter on the edge and knowing he was the only one who could yank her back out of harm's way.

"Lianne is very excited about her new position," Mitch said. "It isn't every day that you're named director of the Honeymoon department."

"Editor," Lianne corrected him.

A slight frown crossed Eunice's face and Lianne could see the wheels turning. The woman could spot relationship problems from a mile away, and right now she was sensing that all was not right in the Cooper household. Lianne's husband didn't even know his wife's proper title!

Lianne quickly stepped to Mitch's side. "Isn't he sweet?" she said, slipping her arm through his. "Honey, Mrs. Pettigrew is the editorial director. I'm just an editor." She forced a bright smile. "A very happily married editor," she added, giving his arm a pat.

"I guess everyone around here is happily married," Mitch said, his gaze shifting to Mrs. Pettigrew.

Lianne saw the look in his eye, that subtle predatory look, one eyebrow quirked up, waiting for an answer he was determined to get. She knew what was coming next. The only thing she *didn't* know was how to stop it.

"Oh, my, yes," the older woman replied. "It's something I take great pride in. Can't you just feel the love in this office? I consider marriage the most honorable and worthy of institutions."

He glanced down at Lianne. "Then you'd never hire a—"

Lianne's pinch stopped his words short. Short of slapping her palm over his mouth, it had been her only option.

"Ouch!" He frowned and rubbed his forearm.

"I'm sorry, sweetheart," Lianne cried. "Did I hurt you?"

"You pinched me," Mitch replied.

"It—it's just that it's nearly noon. If you don't leave now you're going to be late."

His eyes narrowed suspiciously. "Late for what?"

"You know. For that thing you told me about this morning. That *thing* you'll be late for if you don't leave right now."

He frowned, then realization slowly dawned across his handsome features. "Oh, you mean that thing I was supposed to do at noon?" Mitch asked.

Lianne nodded, relieved that he'd decided to play along. Any more of this prevaricating and Mrs. Pettigrew's suspicions would be confirmed. It was time for him to say goodbye. "Yes, *that* thing."

Mitch grinned. "I did that earlier this morning. And now I really don't have anything to do." He shot Mrs. Pettigrew a charming smile. "So being a romantic guy, I decided to stop by and take my wife to lunch."

"What a lovely idea," Eunice said. "So sweet of you, Mitch. It's the little things, the thoughtful gestures, that make a marriage work."

"He is a thoughtful guy," Lianne muttered.

Mitch wrapped his arm around Lianne's shoulders, giving her nothing more to pinch. "We need to discuss our travel plans. I was just telling Mrs. Pettigrew that I thought it would be fun to drive to the mountains rather than fly. A nice long, romantic drive. Don't you think that would be fun, sweetheart?"

Lianne stifled a gasp. "But the Poconos are three hundred miles from Boston." She surreptitiously jabbed her elbow into his ribs. "Dear."

Mrs. Pettigrew's expression brightened. "The mountains are lovely this time of year. The trees won't be turning yet, but the weather should be perfect for a long, leisurely drive. I think Mitchell has a fine idea."

"But we'll need nearly a day to get there and a day to get back. I can't take time from—"

"Of course you can, Lianne," Mrs. Pettigrew interrupted. "You've been working very hard since Cindy left. You deserve a few extra days with your darling husband. Take them. With my blessing."

Lianne groaned inwardly. If spending a week in a hotel room pretending to be Mrs. Mitch Cooper wasn't enough, now she'd be stuck with him for another two days in a car. And just who did he think he was, telling *her* how they'd spend *her* honeymoon?

"We'll take the Mustang," Mitch added. "Driving through the mountains with the top down. You'll like that, won't you, Lianne?"

Actually, Lianne hated driving with the top down, although she'd never actually told Mitch that. She felt vulnerable and unprotected, as if she might just get sucked out of the car when a semitruck drove by.

The convertible top. It was a microcosm of their marriage, both of them subjugating their own personalities for the other; Mitch becoming the perfect lawyer, and

Lianne becoming the perfect wife. Neither one dared to do anything that might rock the proverbial boat. As she looked back on it all now, she saw them both as cardboard cutouts, dull, flat personalities, always smiling through a lifeless marriage, without any real passion between them.

There had been some passion in bed, but even then, it had been so proper and circumspect. Out of the bedroom, they'd been just as proper. In their entire five years together, they'd never fought, not once. Never raised a voice or thrown a dish or slammed a door. The night she'd told him she wanted a divorce, he barely blinked an eye and offered no protest. He'd said that if that was what she wanted, then it was all right with him. That he understood.

She had wanted him to fight, to shout at her and tell her that he'd be damned if he'd let her go. She had wanted him to rage or curse or cry, anything that would reveal his true feelings for her. She had wanted him to tell her that he loved her. But he hadn't. In fact, he'd never once said he loved her, spontaneously, without prompting. He'd always simply followed her own declaration with an "I love you, too, sweetheart," rushing in the phrase, as if saying the words embarrassed him.

At first, it didn't matter. She was certain of his feelings, even if he couldn't bring himself to say it. And then, after she got to know his family, she began to understand. An emotion as deep and personal as love was not something a Cooper talked about. It was assumed that Mitch loved his wife, and that his father loved his mother, and his parents loved Mitch. His entire family was a stew of repressed emotions that weren't allowed to bubble to the surface, a simmering pot of feelings best left unexpressed.

But she had needed him to say the words that night. And when he didn't, she knew she had found her answer. Mitch Cooper had no feelings one way or the other. The marriage had been a mistake.

"Lianne?"

Startled out of her reverie, she blinked, only to find both Mrs. Pettigrew and Mitch waiting for her response. "Why don't we talk about our travel plans at lunch?" she suggested. "I'll just go get my purse and we'll leave."

"I'll wait here," Mitch said.

Lianne looked between Mitch and Mrs. Pettigrew, then decided it might be better to get her "husband" out of danger's way quickly. There was no telling what secrets he might spill under Eunice's careful questioning. "Didn't you say you wanted to see my new office, darling?" She tugged a bit too firmly on his arm. "Come on, I'll show you right now."

Mitch smiled at Mrs. Pettigrew, bid her goodbye, then dutifully followed Lianne into her office. As soon as they were both safely inside, she shut the door behind him and gave his arm another pinch. "What are you doing here?" she demanded, her voice barely above a whisper.

Mitch frowned and rubbed his arm. "What do you think? I came to tell you that I'm ready to accept your offer."

She braced her fists on her hips. "You could have phoned."

"I wanted to see what was so great about this job of yours that you'd be willing to resurrect our marriage to keep it."

"I don't want you around here. There are too many ways you could mess this up for me. When I made this deal, I made it for your body only."

Mitch crooked his eyebrow. "I like the sound of that. But you always told me you married me for my mind. Could it be that you've changed your mind, Annie?"

Lianne felt her cheeks warm. "You know what I mean. I don't need you to meet my boss or make suggestions about how we're going to travel or make any decisions at all. I need you to stand next to me, look like an adoring husband and keep your mouth shut. Understand?"

"Tall, dumb and handsome. That's me." He glanced around the room. "Nice office. You've got a window. You must be important." His gaze stopped at the picture on her desk, their wedding picture. Slowly, he reached out and picked it up. "What's this?"

"Required desktop decoration at *Happily Ever After*," Lianne said. "Everybody has a wedding picture in their office."

"We looked happy," he said softly, rubbing his thumb over the edge of the frame.

Her anger ebbed as she saw a fleeting expression of regret cross his face. "As I remember, we were," she said.

He glanced up. "It wasn't that bad, was it? At least, not all the time."

She nodded. "I think perhaps we were just too young. Both of us were trying so hard to please our families, falling into roles we thought were right for us. No one was at fault. We just grew up."

"I didn't take the picture off *my* desk until three years after you left." He smiled crookedly. "I guess I thought it was...necessary. For my clients. A married lawyer always appears more stable, more trustworthy."

She leaned back on the edge of her desk and crossed her arms in front of her. "Why is that any different from what I'm doing? Pretending to be married to keep my job?"

"I suppose it's not. Except that marriage shouldn't be a requirement for your promotion."

"I have no proof that it is," Lianne said. "It's just a feeling, and having a feeling isn't against the law. So can you just forget you're a lawyer while you're pretending to be my husband?"

He placed the picture back on her desk, then met her gaze. "Only if you forget I made such a mess of our marriage. Only if you'll pretend that we were happy once upon a time."

She reached out and touched his hand, letting her fingers linger on his warm skin for a moment. "We were happy."

He grabbed her hand and wove his fingers through hers. "Why don't we go to lunch, Mrs. Cooper?"

Lianne nodded, then grabbed her purse from the top

of her desk. They strolled down the hall and through the lobby, hand in hand, appearing as comfortable with each other as an old married couple. He stopped at the elevator and turned to her. "By the way, it's your treat for lunch since you've got the better paying job now."

She gave him a sideways glance. "I like this. I call the shots, I pay for lunch, I take you on vacation. And you do exactly what I tell you to do. What more could I want from a husband?"

At times like these, Lianne could almost forget they'd once been married. They seemed like old friends, friends who shared just a tiny bit of sexual attraction between them. Friends who knew exactly what kind of trouble that could cause and were smart enough to bury their attraction.

Perhaps this honeymoon wouldn't be so bad, after all. Perhaps she might even have a little fun.

THEY HOPPED ON THE SUBWAY, then picked up lunch at Quincy Market and walked to Waterfront Park. Mitch listened while Lianne told him about the work she'd do as an editor at *Happily Ever After*. He could see how excited she was, her green eyes bright, her expression focused. In some odd way, it felt good to be able to help her with this, even though her scheme went against every lawyerly instinct he possessed.

In all the time he'd known her, she'd never asked him for anything. Even at the lowest point in their marriage, she hadn't made demands. When he couldn't give her what she wanted, she simply let go. No anger. No recriminations.

They found a ledge overlooking the water and sat down, watching the jets land and take off from the airport across the harbor. A salt-tinged breeze ruffled her honey-colored hair, and she impatiently brushed the strands off her face, then took a bite of her sandwich.

"When do we leave on our honeymoon?" he asked.

She licked a bit of mayonnaise off the corner of her mouth, and he found his gaze fixed on her tongue, wondering if she still tasted as sweet as he remembered from the other day in his apartment. He recalled soft lips, pliant beneath his, her warm breath mingling with his. Such a vivid memory. He dragged his attention away from her mouth, fighting the temptation to kiss her again.

"I was hoping to leave this Sunday, but that doesn't give you much time to get someone to cover your classes for next week."

Mitch shrugged. "That's no problem. I've taken care of it already."

She smiled, surprised and pleased. "Really? Well then, we need to get to work."

He took a long gulp of his lemonade, then wiped his mouth with the back of his hand. "I thought this was supposed to be a vacation."

She shook her head and put her sandwich down between them. "We're supposed to be honeymooners, so we'd better get our stories straight. We were married on Saturday, spent our wedding night in Boston, and then headed to the Poconos for our honeymoon. Other than that, we can pretend that we're us, only ten years ago...but older."

"That's simple enough to remember," he said. "Can I have that pickle?"

"But you're going to have to act like a newlywed instead of my ex-husband."

"And how does a newlywed act?" he asked as he munched on the pickle.

She paused, frowning. "You know. In love. A little dopey. Infatuated with me."

"Horny?" he asked. "I remember feeling that way on our honeymoon."

"No, not horny. Romantic."

"But isn't the purpose of the honeymoon to—"

"Not this honeymoon. This is a working honeymoon. But when we're outside the privacy of our room, you have to act like my husband."

"And you're saying that if I really were your husband, I wouldn't want to jump into bed with you every other minute? I don't think that's very realistic."

"Can we forget this particular characteristic of the ardent honeymooner and move on? I think if you just give me a few long, soulful looks every now and then, you'll make a believable newlywed. You could smile while I speak, take my hand, whisper sweet nothings in my ear. I'm sure that would be plenty to convince anyone."

"What should I whisper?" Mitch asked, enjoying the way her cheeks flushed as he teased her. Why had he never teased before? Lord, she was pretty when she blushed. He could look at her all day and never tire of it.

She sighed in frustration. "I don't know. You'll think of something. Why don't you practice now? First, try giving me a longing look."

Mitch scowled as he struggled to remember if he'd ever given Lianne a longing look and what it felt like. He enjoyed looking at her, but he'd never put a mirror to his face while doing so.

"That's not it."

Concentrating, he tried again to put on a properly lovesick expression. He thought he was doing a pretty good job—until she giggled.

"You look like Irving did after he ate my sofa cushion. Except he was drooling and had foam rubber hanging out of his mouth."

"Why don't we take Irving with us?" Mitch suggested. "I bet he'd enjoy a vacation in the mountains."

She groaned, then shook her head. "This is a perfect example. Why would we want to take a dog on our honeymoon? Is that really what a groom would be thinking about right after his wedding? His dog? Irving is staying with my parents. Now try the look again."

"Maybe it would help if I got in the mood," Mitch suggested, moving closer to her. He slipped his arm around her shoulders and she gave him a suspicious look. "I could kiss you again."

She stiffened. "I—I don't think that would be a good idea. I think it would be best to keep this strictly business."

"And if you thought my adoring look was bad, you ought to see yours right now. Smile, dear. You're supposed to be in love with me."

Lianne moved out of his grasp, then stood up. "I'm sure I'll be able to work up the proper level of enthusiasm when called upon." She glanced at her watch. "I'd better get back to the office."

"You didn't finish your sandwich," Mitch said.

She wrinkled her nose. "You finish it. I'm really not very hungry." Clutching her purse in front of her as if it might offer some protection against him, she shifted uncomfortably. "Sunday," she said.

"You'll pick me up?"

"At 6:00 a.m. sharp."

With that, she gave him a tight smile and started back along the waterfront toward the subway stop. Mitch watched her, wondering what was going through her head, whether she was feeling the attraction that sizzled between them.

Why was it still there, after all these years? Was it the same desire he'd felt on the night he met her, or the day he asked her to marry him? Or was this feeling something different?

As he looked back at what they'd shared, it was as if he'd experienced it with a complete stranger. The Lianne who had sat next to him just a few moments ago wasn't the woman he'd been married to. This Lianne was a woman who teased at his mind and occupied his thoughts, tempting him.

She was his wife, but she wasn't. His feelings for her were supposed to be gone, weakened by the passage of time. But they weren't. They'd come back, like a flash, the instant he'd set eyes on her again. And for the life of him, he wasn't sure what he was going to do about it.

3

"WE'RE LOST."

"I know exactly where we are."

Lianne glared at Mitch from the passenger seat of the Mustang, a crumpled Pennsylvania map spread across her lap. "Then, where are we, Mr. Magellan?"

"I can tell you where we *aren't*. We're not lost. This is the scenic route. Much more interesting than the interstate, don't you think?"

"And we haven't seen a resort in at least an hour. Or a road sign in nearly as long."

"That's the point." Mitch turned to her and smiled, which only served to irritate her more. "Relax, Annie. You're supposed to be looking at the trees and the sky and the wildlife."

"I've had plenty of all three," Lianne replied, clenching her jaw. She reached up and tucked a windblown strand of her hair behind her ear for the millionth time, then slouched down in the seat. And plenty of you, she said to herself.

They'd left Boston early that morning, and from the moment she'd turned the keys of the Mustang over to Mitch, she knew she was in for trouble. First there had been the discussion regarding the convertible top—up or down. He had won that one. Then there was the debate over where to stop for lunch—a nice, safe fast-food place or a truck stop. They dined with at least forty truckers jammed into a tiny greasy spoon. In between, there had been small skirmishes concerning the radio station, the price of gasoline, the combined weight of the luggage she'd brought, and the posted speed limit on New York State highways.

When Mitch decided to venture off the interstate, their civility was all but gone and they'd had a full-blown argument. Of course, he'd won again in convincing fashion. But then, Mitchell Cooper the Third always won. He'd been trained to win from the time he was born. Maybe that's why they'd never argued when they were married—she'd known it would be a lost cause.

All that had changed now. Even though she hadn't won an argument yet, Lianne was determined to make her opinions known. She wasn't the meek little coed he had married, always hoping to please, never rocking the boat. She had changed, and she wasn't about to let Mitch Cooper push her around.

"Stop the car," she demanded.

"Not again," he groaned. "You just had a bathroom break an hour ago. What is it about you women? Can't you plan these—"

"Stop the damn car now!"

For the first time during their trip, Mitch did exactly as he was told. Jamming on the brake, he pulled the car over to the side of the road, shoved it into park, then leaned back in the seat. "There's a nice big rock over there," he suggested.

"Get out."

"I'm not the one who has to go."

She met his incredulous gaze with a steely one of her own. This time she didn't need to speak. He opened the door and stepped out, then crossed his hands over his chest and waited. A satisfied smile curled her lips as she nimbly crawled over the console and settled into the driver's seat.

Lianne ran her hands over the steering wheel and sighed. "This is much better." She turned to him and arched an eyebrow. "Are you going to get back in or will you be walking the rest of the way?"

Grudgingly, Mitch circled the car and got in. "I'm perfectly capable of getting us to the resort."

"I'm sure you are, Mitch. But I was hoping to get there before we had to check out next Saturday. I have a job to do."

"It's 2:48," Mitch said, glancing at his watch. "You wanted to be there by three."

"And we're lost," she repeated.

"Don't you trust me, Annie?"

She gave him a sideways glance. "I hate it when you call me Annie. It makes me sound like that naive girl you married. Call me Lianne."

"You didn't answer my question, *Lianne*," he said. "I asked if you trusted me."

"It's not a question of trust," she said, evading the question. She did trust Mitch. She'd always trusted him, always knew that no matter what had passed between them, she could come to him for help. Perhaps she had known all along that he would help her with her plan and that's why she'd gone to his apartment that day.

Mitch had always been one of the good guys. That's why she'd fallen in love with him in the first place. She recalled the moment he'd stepped up to the library's circulation desk. A sophomore at B.U., she'd worked two part-time jobs. One of them in the law library. He'd been in his first year of law school and she'd helped him search for an obscure book on ethics. At the end of the search he'd asked her out for coffee.

Back then, he'd been conservative, stable and steady, a man any mother would want for a son-in-law, a man who would never just up and quit his job. Those qualities had made up for the emotional distance he seemed to maintain from those around him. They had also made him a great lawyer.

But something had changed for him—or in him—and she wasn't sure what it was. Whatever had kept him buttoned up so tight had loosened a bit and revealed a different man beneath, someone reckless and a bit cynical.

Regardless of what it was that had made him leave the family firm, it must have been a difficult decision for him. He'd always believed he could make a difference in the world from behind a desk at Cooper, Cooper and Cooper. And in the five years of their marriage, he had sacrificed everything, including their marriage, to do just that.

She had gradually seen the idealism fade from his eyes as he put in hour after hour at the office. He'd become preoccupied and distant, and before she knew it, the pressures of his work had spilled over into their personal lives.

She'd allowed it to happen as much as he had. She could have stood up and fought for what she wanted, but Mitch had no longer been the man she'd fallen in love with. Nor was she the woman he'd married. It seemed simpler and less hurtful to walk away.

But now, as she spent more time with him, she wondered if they could have worked through their problems. If they could have made it through the hard times together.

She cursed silently. Second-guessing the past was not a practical use of her time. She had put all those feelings far behind her. Mitch was no longer her husband, though they'd spend the next week pretending otherwise. And any thoughts she had of rekindling what they'd shared were pure folly.

"Yes," she said softly. "I trust you. Except in matters of highway navigation."

He reached over and tucked a wind-whipped strand of hair behind her ear. "Good," he said, allowing his fingers to linger for a moment on her cheek. "I'd never do anything to hurt you, Lianne."

She was afraid to look at him, afraid of what she might see in his eyes. So instead, she kept her attention focused on the road ahead, slowing for a stop sign.

The road they had been on came to an end, and Lianne looked left and then right. "Which way?"

Mitch shrugged, grinning. "You're the driver, sweetheart. I'm going wherever you take me."

"I'm turning left," she said.

"I'd go right," Mitch countered.

"Who's driving?"

"You are. But if I were you, I'd still go right. It's just down the road."

She looked in that direction, but couldn't see anything but tall trees and a curving highway.

"Trust me," he said. "Just this once. If you turn right, we'll be there before three o'clock."

Lianne laughed. "All right. This I have to see. And if it's not there?"

"It will be," Mitch assured her. "I told you I'd get you to the resort in time."

"If it's not there, I get to keep the Mustang for another month." She expected him to refuse the wager, to take the sure thing, his beloved car. He'd always played it safe, always made the prudent choice. But instead, he grinned wickedly and agreed.

"And what if you lose?" he asked.

"I've already wagered my car and part of my dog," Lianne protested. "What more can you take from me?"

"There is one thing." He paused, then reached out and turned her to face him, resting his fingers gently on her chin. "If you lose, I get a kiss. Just one. On demand. Whenever and wherever I ask for it. With no complaints."

Lianne considered the wager for a moment, then reluctantly nodded. What did she really have to lose? In all honesty, she'd thought a lot about kissing him lately. And if the kiss was simply to settle a bet, she'd be certain to keep any desire to a minimum. "You're not going to win," she warned.

"I wouldn't have taken the bet if I had any doubt," he replied.

She swung the car out onto the road, following his directions. A few moments later, a sign appeared out of the foliage beside the road.

"Pocono Pines Honeymoon Resort," Mitch read smugly. "I believe that's where we're going, isn't it? One mile to the left."

THE NARROW ROAD into the resort wound through the thick woods until all at once, the trees thinned and the sunlight broke through the leafy cover. In front of them, an immense two-story lodge stood on a rise above a shimmering crystal lake. Behind the building, Lianne could see cabins set in the woods, some scattered down to the shore. A deep veranda spanned the length of the lodge, lined with rough-hewn Adirondack chairs.

It was a place of honeymoon dreams, peaceful and secluded, and wonderfully romantic. She fought back a flood of delicious anticipation. This was work, not a real honeymoon, and the man who sat beside her was merely a stand-in husband. "It's beautiful," she murmured.

"I wonder if there are any fish in that lake," Mitch replied, his interest focused on the water.

Her grip tightened on the steering wheel. "Is that all you can think about?" she asked.

"It's just that I've never been fishing. I thought I might give it a try."

"This is supposed to be our honeymoon. Remember

what we discussed? Your attention should be focused on your new bride, not on a bunch of silly fish."

"Yes, darling," he said in a teasing tone.

Lianne parked the Mustang in front of the lodge, and they'd both barely stepped out of the car when a slender woman rushed down the front steps, a clipboard clutched in her hand. She was perfectly tanned, her platinum blond pageboy cut creating a striking contrast against her sun-darkened skin and her white Pocono Pines shirt and khaki shorts.

"You must be the Coopers!" she cried. "We've been waiting for you. I'm Clarissa Bliss, activities director at the Pocono Pines. I'm here to make your honeymoon perfect." She gave them both a hug, accompanied by a dazzling smile. "Aren't you just the cutest couple!"

Lianne opened her mouth to speak, but Clarissa continued.

"We have a host of activities for you here at the resort." Her hands shuffled through the papers on the clipboard. "Golf, hiking, horseback riding, sailing, tennis, volleyball, waterskiing. Plus many team sports like baseball and basketball."

"Fishing?" Mitch asked.

Clarissa nodded enthusiastically. "Of course. In the lake and in several nearby streams. We'd be happy to equip you both with whatever you need. We also have ballroom dancing lessons, gourmet cooking classes, wine-tasting seminars. We have a fitness center and spa, with saunas and steam baths. And a wonderful dining room with nightly entertainment. You're in the Summit cabin, which is our very finest accommodation. This is your free honeymoon album and your activities schedule. I don't seem to have your Happy Honeymooner profiles here." She handed a stack of paperwork to Lianne. "We absolutely must have that completed so we can help make your honeymoon the best it can be. And that's your resort map and table assignment for dinner. I've put you with a lovely couple, Kip and Kelly Jean Albright. This is a reservation card for your complimentary champagne breakfast in bed. Just turn that in the evening before."

Lianne struggled to keep all the papers in order, then finally shoved them all at Mitch.

Clarissa checked her clipboard again, the picture of efficiency, then snapped her manicured fingers. A young man, dressed in the same uniform as Clarissa, appeared on the veranda. "James will take your luggage to your cabin and park your car. If you'll follow me, I'll get you registered and signed up for tomorrow's activities. You can fill out your Happy Honeymooner profiles right away." She spun on her heel and hurried up the steps, leaving Lianne and Mitch to stare after her.

"This should be fun," Mitch murmured, slipping his arm around Lianne's waist and drawing her closer. He bent down, his breath teasing at her hair. "When am I supposed to find time to whisper all those sweet nothings in your ear?"

She turned toward him and forced a smile, well aware of the warmth of his hand resting on her hip, the closeness of his mouth to hers. "Just be careful," she said.

But as they followed Clarissa Bliss up to the front entrance of the lodge, Lianne wondered if she was the one who should be taking care. She'd come to anticipate his touch more than she wanted. And there would be more than enough time over the next week for her defenses to be tested.

He's not my husband, she said to herself over and over again. *And I'm not in love with him. Not anymore.*

If she couldn't remember that, this make-believe honeymoon could turn into a bigger disaster than her marriage.

MITCH PRESSED a five-dollar bill into the bellhop's hand, then closed the front door behind him. The sound of the latch clicking echoed through the silence of the cabin, and Lianne felt herself stiffen slightly. They'd been alone all day in the car, but somehow, being alone in a romantic honeymoon cabin was much more disconcerting.

"So," he murmured, "here we are."

She cleared her throat, then glanced nervously around the sitting room, trying hard to act indifferent. "Yes, here we are. It—it's a lovely cabin, don't you think?" She drew in a deep breath, then reached inside her purse and pulled out a small notepad. "I should really record my first impressions."

"Lovely," Mitch replied with a chuckle. "That's not exactly my first impression of the place."

The front door opened into a plush sitting room with a fieldstone fireplace on one end and a heart-shaped whirlpool tub, set against tall windows, on the other.

Above the tub was a sleeping loft, again with a wall of windows, and from where she stood, Lianne could see that the shape of the bed was the same as the tub. Though rustic in decor, all the amenities made it a very luxurious hideaway for a honeymoon couple.

"I'm not interested in your impressions," Lianne said.

"Don't you think it's a little...obvious? A den of iniquity nestled among the pines." He strolled across the room and peered into the whirlpool tub. "Made for two," he commented. "And I'd be willing to bet there are mirrors above the bed. The whole place just shouts 'Let's get down to it, baby.'"

"I'll be sure to note that in my review," she said dryly. "'The accommodations shout sex.'"

"Perhaps your readers might enjoy a firsthand account of how the tub works. Care to join me?"

Lianne shook her head slowly. "Don't get any ideas," she reminded him. "This is strictly business, Mitch Cooper." She paused. "So, I suppose you want your kiss now."

Mitch walked to the door and picked up his duffel bag. "Naw. That can wait. We've got plenty of time. I'll just settle myself upstairs while you take the couch." He pushed down on one of the cushions as he passed. "It looks fairly comfortable. But if it bothers you, you're always welcome to share the bed."

"I don't intend to spend any more time with you than I have to," Lianne said.

He stepped in front of her and bent closer. "You don't know how talk like that excites me, Annie. My new bride is utterly repulsed by me. I should be crushed, heartbroken. But I'm not."

Lianne swallowed hard, her gaze transfixed by his. Repulsed? She was far from repulsed by Mitch Cooper. The truth be told, she'd had to stop herself from dwelling on the features of his face, on the tempting way his dark hair curled over his shirt collar, on the perfect blue of his eyes. Her attention dropped to his mouth, his exquisitely chiseled lips, curved slightly at the corners. She wanted him to kiss her again, to collect on his bet and more. As he leaned a little closer, she closed her eyes, waiting.

"I love a challenge," he murmured. "And you, dear wife, are definitely a challenge," he added in a flippant tone.

Lianne's eyes snapped back open.

He pinched her chin playfully, then crossed the room to the loft stairs. "By the way, I signed up for a wilderness horseback ride tomorrow and a rock climb the day after that. I expect I'll be gone all day, so you'll have plenty of time to work on your article."

Lianne gasped. "What?" Her voice sounded a little too shrill, even to her ears.

Mitch turned and frowned. "I thought you'd be happy. I'll be out from underfoot."

"But—but this is supposed to be our honeymoon," she sputtered, attempting to regain her composure. "We're supposed to spend time together. All our time. Every minute."

"You just said—"

"Forget what I just said. There's a big difference between what goes on in this room and the picture of marital happiness we have to present outside. Everything we do has to be done as a couple. You'll just have to cancel your plans."

Mitch dropped his bag on the stairs and leaned casually against the newel post. Her gaze drifted down his body, past his slim hips and down his long legs. Lord, when had he learned to wear a pair of jeans so well? She'd never been one to focus on the physical, but it was hard not to with Mitch in the room.

"This is new," he commented.

"What?"

"I've never seen this side of you, Annie. So stubborn and outspoken. You were always so sweet and accommodating. What happened?"

She tipped her chin up defiantly. "I'm not the woman you married, and the sooner you realize that, the better. Are you going to cancel?"

"No," Mitch said. "I'm not. You'll just have to accompany your husband like any dutiful wife would. I've always wanted to learn to ride, and I told Clarissa Bliss that you were very excited about the prospect of learning to scale a sheer cliff."

"I am not your dutiful little wife!"

Mitch grinned. "Yes, you are. You forget, we were just married yesterday. You're madly in love with me, and your only thoughts at this moment are of how much you want to make me happy. If you were my bride, sweetheart, you'd bury your fears and learn to ride horses and climb rocks. To please your husband."

She ground her teeth as she glared at him. "This is

nothing more than blackmail. It's nasty and unethical—and not at all like the Mitch Cooper I used to know."

He hefted his bag up from the stair, then shrugged. "You're the one who made this deal, Annie. I'm just along for the ride. And I intend to make that ride interesting." He turned and made his way up to the sleeping loft.

When he disappeared from view, Lianne cursed softly, then turned and walked out the front door, slamming it behind her. "This is not fair," she muttered, pacing the length of the porch. "He's getting the car and the dog *and* a free vacation. But if I don't do things his way, he's going to blow my whole plan right out of the water. I don't know what more he wants. The man is going to drive me crazy!"

"You can't be talking about your husband!"

Lianne glanced down to find a petite brunette watching her with wide eyes. She raised an eyebrow. "I can't? And why not?"

"Because you're on your honeymoon, silly." The perky cheerleader-type rushed up onto the porch and held out her hand. "I just couldn't wait until dinner to meet you, so I came right over. I'm Kelly Jean Albright. And you must be Lianne Cooper. Miss Bliss told me you just got here. I wanted to come over right away and introduce myself. I would have brought my husband, Kip, but he went fishing. He just loves to fish. He's been fishing since we arrived. Though I can't understand the allure." She stopped suddenly, then giggled. "Allure! Oh, that's funny. I'll have to remember to tell Kip. A lure. Get it?"

Lianne forced a smile. Terminally perky. As if her "honeymoon" wasn't going badly enough already!

"Does your husband like to fish?" Kelly Jean babbled. "If he does, he should go with Kip. Kip just loves to fish." She giggled again. "But then, I told you that already. Well, if they went fishing together, at least you and I could spend some time together. Wouldn't that be nice? I'd love to hear all about your wedding. Every detail. Tell me about your dress. Do you have pictures?"

"My dress?"

"Yes, silly, your dress. Was it the most beautiful thing you've ever worn? Did you feel like a fairy princess? It took me two years to find the perfect bridal gown. What was yours like?"

"I really don't remember," Lianne said distractedly.

"You don't remember?" Kelly Jean laughed this time, a sound that immediately had the ability to set Lianne's nerves on edge and send the wildlife running. "You must remember. You just had it on yesterday, didn't you?"

"It was white," Lianne said, scrambling to cover such an obvious blunder. "And it had a lot of lace and some seed pearls. And a full skirt."

"And how long was your train? Mine was six feet. I wanted a ten-foot train, but Kip said absolutely not. He wasn't going to put up with me dragging my dress up the aisle. He can be so bossy sometimes. But what can I say? I love him to death. Where's your husband?"

"He's inside. Unpacking." Lianne glanced over her shoulder and smiled wanly. "Maybe I should go inside and help."

Kelly Jean grabbed her hand to stop her. "Don't go, silly. Kip would never dream of unpacking for me. Your husband must love you very much." A rueful expression crossed her features, but then it was quickly replaced with an overbright smile. "The next time there's unpacking to be done, I'm going to insist that Kip do it." She covered her mouth, as if her declaration might be overheard. "Or maybe not."

Lianne groaned inwardly as titles for her Poconos honeymoon article raced through her mind. Escape to the Poconos had quickly turned to Run Screaming from the Poconos. And Honeymoon from Hell would sum up her experience perfectly so far. She could hardly wait to add the absent and seemingly overbearing Kip to the mix.

"Hear that?" Lianne cocked her head. "I think that's my husband calling."

"I was supposed to wait on the dock for Kip. He wants me to take a picture of him with those smelly old fish. I should probably go, too." Kelly Jean sighed in disappointment. "We'll have more time to talk at dinner tonight. I've just got oodles to tell you. And I know Kip will want to meet your husband."

"I don't think we'll be—"

"You have to come to dinner!" Kelly Jean cried. "Miss Bliss tells me that we have a lot in common. Your Mitch is a lawyer with his family's firm and so is Kip! Can you believe that? It must be fate that we both came here for our honeymoon. And she said you have a degree in journalism. I was a broadcast major before we got married. I wanted to be a weather girl."

"You mean a meteorologist?" Lianne asked.

"Oh, no. Just a weather girl. I'm no good at science. Kip says I'd be good at predicting wind speed since the breeze just blows in one ear and out the other." She demonstrated with a dopey smile and two fingers. "But now, I just want to be the best wife I can."

Kelly Jean's goal sounded painfully familiar to Lianne. She'd said those same words to her mother just before *her* wedding. Time after time, her mother had warned her that marrying into a wealthy Boston family would be difficult for her. That she would spend many lonely hours while Mitch's attention was occupied elsewhere. And Lianne had replied that she'd only need to be the best wife she could be and all would turn out just fine.

It hadn't. And now, as she listened to Kelly Jean babble on about her cooking lessons and her volunteer work, she could see herself ten years ago, trapped in the town house on Beacon Hill, waiting for all the happiness to begin. She'd been so naive about what it took to make a marriage work. So hopeful that she would beat the odds—totally blind to all the troubles that lay in wait.

She fought the urge to sit Kelly Jean down on the front porch of the cabin and fill her in on the realities of marriage. Especially marriage to a man who couldn't even unpack his own bags. A man who spent his honeymoon sitting in a boat in the middle of the lake while his wife was starved for company.

But Kelly Jean's happiness was not her concern. Lianne was here to do a job, and that job did not include marriage counseling. Besides, if she'd had any talent at the institution of marriage, she wouldn't be pretending to be happily wedded to a man she'd divorced five years ago.

She hesitated before making one final attempt to escape. Talking to Kelly Jean would probably be safer than spending time alone in the cabin with Mitch, a whirlpool tub and a heart-shaped bed. But in the end, she made up a feeble excuse about missing the sign-up deadline for cooking classes. She headed toward the lodge, with Kelly Jean hard on her heels, determined to sign up for the same classes. Perhaps she should have taken her chances with Mitch, Lianne mused, listening to Kelly Jean chatter about the menus at her wedding reception.

With Mitch, there was always the chance that he might collect on the kiss she owed him. And that possibility was infinitely more interesting than anything Kelly Jean Albright had to say.

"HE'S A BOOR," Lianne said.

"She's an airhead," Mitch countered, pulling Lianne closer to him as they walked along the lake. Like most of the other couples at the resort, they had dined at an extravagant buffet dinner, then wandered outside to watch the sun set over the water.

Lianne stiffened beside him, but Mitch refused to allow her to push away. She was the one who wanted a perfect picture of marital bliss, and he was merely obliging. Besides, he liked the feel of her beneath his arm, the smell of her hair and the warmth of her body against his. He slid his hand down her spine, lingering over the gentle curve at the small of her back.

"Kelly Jean is *not* an airhead," Lianne protested. "Besides, she only acts that way because it's the role he's forced her into. If he weren't such an arrogant ass, she wouldn't have to play dumb."

"Sweetheart, I think you better face the truth about your new friend. Kelly Jean is a nitwit. The poor thing flunked out of weather girl school."

"She left college to marry Kip. And she's not my friend. She's just an...acquaintance."

"Exactly my point. So why are you defending her?"

Lianne twisted away from him and put a few inches between them. "And why are you defending him?"

"I like the guy. He reminds me of me, a few years ago. Out to save the world. All full of himself. Just a tad arrogant."

"Well, I just think he could be more considerate."

Mitch sighed and shook his head. "Could we just forget about Kelly Jean and Kip for a little while?"

She took his advice and didn't say another word, preferring to stare out at the lake, her arms crossed beneath her breasts. He hadn't realized how much he needed to touch her until she stepped away from him. Funny how he couldn't recall ever feeling that way when they'd been married, ever having such an overpowering urge to take her in his arms and explore her body with his hands. Maybe if he had touched her more...

Mitch cursed silently. *Maybe.* He'd been using that word a lot lately. If he hadn't been obsessed with work, maybe. If he'd paid more attention to Lianne's needs, maybe. It was too late for maybes. He'd had his chance with her and he'd blown it. And he knew, there wouldn't be another one. Lianne had changed, and she certainly didn't need him to make her happy.

"She should stand up to him," Lianne said, interrupting his thoughts. "If she doesn't, she'll start to resent him. He'll put in longer and longer hours at the office. She'll sit at home, wondering whether she made a mistake. After a while, they won't be able to stand the sight of each other."

Mitch pulled back and looked down into her eyes. "Are you still talking about Kelly Jean and Kip? Or are you talking about us?"

She shifted uneasily, then averted her gaze. "I'm just saying that Kelly Jean had better find herself a backbone or Kip is going to trample all over her."

"Is that what I did to you, Lianne?"

"We're not talking about us," she reminded him. "I think I'm going to sit down with Kelly Jean and have a little woman-to-woman talk. Tell her how it is."

"Don't get involved in their marriage," Mitch warned.

"Kelly Jean might benefit from a little bit of my wisdom."

"What wisdom? We just got married ourselves, or have you forgotten?"

"Then you can talk to Kip. Go fishing with him. Tell him to go a little easier on Kelly Jean. He should let her be herself. He shouldn't try to turn her into something she isn't."

She looked so pretty, standing in the light of the setting sun, her skin burnished golden and her hair fiery from the reflection off the lake. He studied her mouth for a long moment, wondering if he should collect his kiss now, already anticipating the taste and feel of her lips beneath his. Desire knifed through him, the dull ache settling in his gut. He clenched his fists behind his back and staved it off.

If he kissed her now, that would be the end of it, nothing more than a wager settled. And he wanted their kiss to be more, to lead to the desire that had sparked between them the last time he'd touched her lips. If he resisted temptation and marshaled his patience, he might be able to knock down a few more of those barriers she'd set up between them.

"Let Kip and Kelly Jean work out their own problems. If their marriage wasn't meant to be, it wasn't meant to be. It's as simple as that."

She stared up at him, astonished. "How can you say that?" Quickly, she held up her hand to stop his reply. "Never mind. I know exactly how. In fact, I've experienced it firsthand."

"And what is that?"

"Your indifference regarding marriage. Your willingness to give up rather than fight for our relationship."

"So we *are* talking about us now," Mitch said, his words laced with cynicism.

"No!" She cursed softly. "Yes, maybe we are."

"You're the one who wanted the divorce, Lianne, not me."

"You could have refused. You could have asked me to stay."

"Why? So I could have had the pleasure of making you even more miserable than you already were? So I could see every day how I'd failed you? I didn't want that, and I don't think you did, either."

"You just let me walk out," she said, the hurt so evident in her voice, it made his chest ache with regret. "If you had loved me, you would have found a way to make me stay."

He sucked in a sharp breath, then held it, fighting the anger and remorse that ate at his soul. "I could have," he murmured.

She bit her bottom lip. "Didn't you want me to stay? Didn't you love me even a little bit?"

Her voice was thin and vulnerable, and he knew how much courage it took for her to ask. He'd asked himself the same questions over and over again, and he always came up with the same answers.

"No," he replied, steeling himself against the flash of pain in her eyes. "I didn't want you to stay. And I didn't love you the way you deserved to be loved."

She straightened her spine and composed herself, putting on an indifferent expression. "I appreciate your honesty," she said in a tight tone. She rubbed her fingers over her forehead distractedly, then looked up at him. "It's been a long day and I'm really tired. I think I'll turn in now."

"I'll walk with you back to the cabin."

She shook her head. "No, I'm fine. I can find my way on my own. Besides, I could use some time to myself."

Mitch reached out and took her hand, twisting his fingers through hers so she couldn't pull away. "You take the bed," he said. "You'll be more comfortable. And that way I won't wake you when I come in."

She shook her head. "No, a deal's a deal. I'll sleep on the couch." She paused, her gaze nervously flitting around. "Good night, Mitch," she said, her eyes fixed somewhere near his shoulder.

He dropped her hand. "Good night, Annie. Sleep well."

She nodded, then turned and walked toward their cabin. He watched her in the low light, cursing himself and his misplaced honesty. He should have told her what she wanted to hear, that he'd had his reasons for letting her go. That he had loved her but couldn't bring himself to ask her to stay. Hell, how could he have believed she loved him when he had so completely loathed himself?

Mitch raked his hands through his hair, staring at the place where she'd disappeared into the woods. He hadn't known it at the time, but the end of their marriage was just the beginning of a long and painful part of his professional life, a time he would just as soon forget.

But now that Lianne had come back, all the old memories had returned, all the regrets and the questions. He'd thought he had put them all behind him when he left the firm, but he'd merely walked away from them. The memories would always be there.

When the case had first landed on his desk, he had almost taken a pass, preferring to give it to one of the associates. But after reviewing the file, he knew he could settle quickly and cleanly, without major financial damage to his client. Just another in a long line of product liability suits that Cooper, Cooper and Cooper deftly defended for their wealthy, and sometimes negligent, clients.

But this case had been different. It involved an injury to a child, an injury that couldn't be fixed by money alone. The case dragged on and on in the courts as he filed motion after motion until the family was nearly broke with the medical bills.

The more time he spent on the case, the more he came to hate the role he played, protecting the guilty at the expense of an innocent little boy. The tension at the office followed him home and spilled into his marriage. And when Lianne had asked for a divorce, he came to the realization that he was no longer the man she married. He was a man she had every reason to detest.

When Lianne walked out, he threw himself into his work, taking on a more demanding caseload in an attempt to forget the one case that plagued his mind. Appeals were filed, and still the case dragged on.

Then one day, it was over. He'd won. He'd kept his client from any financial responsibility to the child, and he finally thought he would be able to sleep at night.

But still, the thoughts of that child, the injuries and the long and expensive rehabilitation would not leave him, and he came to loathe himself and the role he had played.

It had been just over a year ago, on a morning not much different from any other workday morning. He'd walked into his family's bank and had withdrawn every cent of his trust fund, close to $500,000. He cut a cashier's check to the child's parents for the same amount, and then stuffed the check in an envelope and dropped it into the mailbox.

The story made the evening news the next day, an anonymous donor, a relieved family, a child with at least a fighting chance to live a normal life. He'd sat in front of the television and watched as a great weight lifted off his chest. He could finally breathe again, and with every breath, a small bit of his self-respect returned.

His father had been so smug, so righteous, as if the anonymous donor had somehow absolved the firm of any responsibility.

It took three days for Mitchell Cooper the Second to learn of the raid on his son's trust fund. Mitch wasn't surprised, considering his father served on the board of the bank. An argument ensued, and in the end Mitch had walked out the doors of Cooper, Cooper and Cooper, vowing never to return.

The decision had changed his life, not just from a financial standpoint—it had changed the very essence of who he was. For the first time in a long time, he respected himself. He had acted out of pure bone-deep emotion and it had felt good.

Mitch stared out across the lake, now dark with the reflection of the evening sky, then turned and started toward the cabin. Was that what he was doing here with Lianne? Acting on his emotions? Or was he letting his emotions run away with him?

She didn't love him anymore, and any thought he had of changing that fact was pure foolishness. Yet he couldn't get her out of his head. Old feelings and new feelings mixed together until he couldn't push them aside. Hell, he didn't want to push them aside. He wanted to savor them, to linger over each and every flood of desire that shot through him.

He smiled to himself. He had become infatuated with his ex-wife, fascinated by a woman who had walked out of his life five years ago. And though he wasn't quite sure what he wanted to do about it, he was sure that something interesting was bound to happen during their week at the Pocono Pines.

4

A ROMANTIC, DAYLONG trail ride. Or that's what the brochure had described. But Lianne could find nothing romantic about getting up at dawn, climbing on top of a crabby old nag and following a dusty trail of chipper honeymooners into the woods. There was no way this part of the honeymoon would receive a favorable review.

She reached up and rubbed her eyes, then wrinkled her nose at the horsey smell that seemed to have transferred itself from the animal to her. Perhaps she wasn't in the best mood to render an objective viewpoint. She hadn't slept well last night, tossing and turning on the sofa, listening for every sound that came from the sleeping loft above.

Jumbled images of Mitch lying alone, naked, in the heart-shaped bed teased at her mind, and she'd wondered if he was wide-awake, as she was. She'd heard him come in and had pinched her eyes shut as he'd approached the sofa. Holding her breath, she had tried not to move when he pulled the comforter up to her chin, all the while feeling his presence above her.

She waited for his touch, anticipated it, hoping it would give her a reason to open her eyes. But then he had turned and his footsteps disappeared up the loft stairs. She wasn't sure when she finally fell asleep, but she was certain that her dreams had been plagued with the same images—flashes of Mitch mixed with nagging desire.

The next thing she knew, he was shouting at her from the loft railing, his hair wet from the shower, his naked chest gleaming with a fine sheen of moisture. She tumbled out of bed, got dressed and followed him numbly out the door. That's how she'd ended up here—on the trail.

She'd already been whacked in the face twice by vicious tree branches, nearly been bitten by her horse a dozen times and had almost tumbled off the saddle in an attempt to keep an eye on Mitch. Since she'd drawn the least cooperative of the horses, a disinterested mare named Daisy, she also now lagged well behind the group. Even Kip and Kelly Jean, who'd decided to tag along, had shown better equestrian skills. But then, Kip seemed to know everything about horses and riding, just as he knew everything about everything else. And Kelly Jean put on a happy face simply to impress her husband.

As for Lianne, she didn't give a damn if Mitch knew she was miserable. This whole thing was his fault! Shifting on the saddle, she rubbed her sore backside, all the while cursing his enthusiasm for new experiences. An entire day on the back of a horse? He'd never shown the least interest in outdoor activities when they'd been married. His idea of the great outdoors was a barbecue at his parents' country club.

But he'd certainly taken to riding—and to the pretty

riding instructor at the head of the trail. Lianne peered around the other horses, trying to catch a glimpse of him, sliding one foot out of the stirrup to get a better angle. He was too far ahead. She stretched a bit farther, and an instant later she felt herself slipping, listing off to one side of the saddle. Frantic for a handhold, she knew she was in trouble.

The rocky ground passed by below her as the nag continued to plod along, unaware of her predicament. Lianne reached up for the saddle horn, but her fingers were hopelessly tangled in the reins. With a cry of dismay, she hit the ground, her right foot still caught in the stirrup. Her horse stopped immediately, then turned around and began to nibble on her jacket sleeve as if she were merely some stray bit of alfalfa.

"Stop it!" she hissed, slapping at the mare's nose. Twisting her foot, she finally extricated herself from the stirrup, only to have Daisy continue plodding down the trail on her own. When she scrambled to catch her, the horse took off at a trot.

"That's fine!" she shouted at Daisy's retreating rump. "I'd rather walk, anyway." Lianne tried to push herself up from the ground, but she'd landed hard on her hip and a sharp pain shot down her leg. Perhaps a rest might be in order. She'd catch up to Daisy in a few minutes. Besides, the horse was too lazy to go far.

With a groan, she flopped back onto the trail and covered her eyes with her arms. What had ever given her the idea that this honeymoon would be relaxing? From the time they'd arrived, there had been one problem or another to deal with, and every one had Mitch Cooper's name written all over it.

It wouldn't be so hard to deal with if he wasn't so damn irresistible, so incredibly sexy. Every time she got angry, he managed to turn on the charm until all she could think about was touching him or kissing him or burying her face in his muscled chest. Even the thought of it now brought a warm flush to her cheeks.

Lianne sighed and rubbed at her dust-reddened eyes. "Get a hold of yourself," she murmured. "Just take a moment to relax and put everything in perspective."

But a few moments later, the rapid thud of approaching hoofs brought her bolting upright. Instinctively, she rolled off the trail and covered her head, expecting Daisy to come racing through and trample her to death. The nag was nothing more than the devil in horse's clothing, determined to stomp her flat if she couldn't eat her.

"Geez, Annie, what happened? Are you all right?"

Hesitantly, she peeked up to find Mitch hovering over her.

"We stopped to set up for lunch, and your horse came trotting along without you." He slid off his saddle and bent down beside her. "Are you hurt? Is anything broken? Can you stand?"

She slapped at the hand he offered. "Of course I can stand!" Every muscle in her body ached, but she managed to drag herself upright in time for Kip and Kelly Jean's hasty arrival. A few moments later, the riding instructor was standing in the midst of the group, a look of concern on her pretty features. They all began to babble at once, and Lianne covered her ears and shook her head.

"I'm perfectly fine," she assured them. "I just got off to take a little break and my horse walked away, that's all." She forced a smile. "When I tried to catch her, she ran. I'm not hurt. Go on, get back to lunch, I'll catch up." She shooed them off, and they all reluctantly left, except for Mitch.

Without warning, he dragged her into his arms and hugged her tight, pressing his lips against her forehead. "You scared the hell out of me. I saw that horse and then you, lying on the trail. I imagined all sorts of things, the worst of which I don't even want to say."

She wriggled out of his embrace. "They're gone, Mitch. You don't have to play the concerned husband anymore."

He met her gaze, frowning, then cursed beneath his breath. "Damn it, I'm not playacting. Is it so hard to believe that I was worried?"

She gave him a sulky look, one he fully deserved. "I think your mind was on other things—or should I say, another woman—other than your wife, that is. So just how do you plan to handle your interest in our riding instructor? Are you going to meet her behind the lodge after dark?"

Impatiently, Mitch grabbed her by the arm and spun her around, then began to brush the dirt off her jacket and the seat of her jeans. "My interest?" He chuckled and slapped a little too hard on her backside. "If I didn't know better, I'd say you were jealous." He peered over her shoulder, his breath teasing at her ear. "Are you jealous, Annie?"

She twisted away from him and rubbed her hands where his had been, trying to forget how delicious it felt to have him touch her, to have him so close, so concerned. "Of her? Why should I be? You're a single man. You're perfectly able to associate with whatever women interest you. I just don't want you to blow our cover by involving us both in some silly extramarital flirtation."

"I was just talking to her about horses, nothing more. I thought you were right behind us. The next thing I knew, your horse came trotting up to me." He reached out and gently pushed the hair out of her eyes, catching her gaze with his. "I'm not interested in anyone but you, Lianne."

A shiver skittered down her spine at the simple, heartfelt honesty in his eyes, and for a moment, she thought he'd truly meant what he'd said. But then she realized Mitch was simply playing his role. "That *is* the deal," she murmured.

He blinked, then looked away, his jaw tight. "Yes," he said, an unexpected trace of sarcasm in his voice. "That's the deal. Don't worry, I haven't forgotten."

"And you'd better not," she said lamely, surprised at the sudden tension she saw in his expression. She straightened her jacket and tucked her hair behind her ear. "I guess we'd better catch up with the others. The sooner we eat, the sooner this ride will be over."

She took a step, then winced at the ache that twisted along her leg. She'd probably have a huge bruise tomorrow, but luckily she hadn't broken any bones. Rubbing her hip, Lianne hobbled off down the trail with Mitch at her side. A strained silence grew between them as they both stared straight ahead.

Her mind returned again and again to his words and the foolish impulse that made her want to believe them. Mitch was *pretending* to care about her, merely acting the part of a concerned lover. Any fantasies she had in the other direction were simply that—fantasies. Fantasies she had no business entertaining.

They were nearly in sight of the others, gathered around a blazing campfire built in a clearing beside the trail, when Mitch put his arm around her shoulders and gave her a gentle hug. "Are you sure you're all right? We can go back to the cabin if you'd like."

"I'm hungry, and after four solid hours on that ridiculous excuse for a horse, I'm not anxious to get back on. Besides, I think it would look better if we stayed."

"I'm sorry I made you come along," he said. "I guess I should have known horses weren't your thing. But you've got to admit that we've seen some incredible scenery."

She gave him a sideways glance and smiled grudgingly. "It was a new experience. Now I can say I've ridden a horse. I can also say I've fallen off a horse. But I'll tell you right now, after this, I'm not going rock climbing. You can forget that right now."

He wove his fingers through the hair at the nape of her neck, and a warm shiver worked its way through her body. "I can try to change your mind, can't I?" His fingers gently massaged her nape.

Lianne fought the impulse to melt right there on the trail and instead narrowed her eyes in warning. She could not, and would not, allow herself to be swayed by his charm!

"You could come along and watch?"

She shook her head. "There are other things we can do together, Mitch. They don't all have to involve risking life and limb. From now on, all extra activities are cleared through me. Understand? Besides, I need to write a balanced article about this place."

"And I guess you can't do that from a hospital bed, right?"

A laugh burst from her throat at the mock seriousness in his voice, and she gave him a playful shove as they negotiated a muddy part of the trail. When had he developed a sense of humor?

She picked up her pace a bit, satisfied that she'd finally straightened him out. The rest of the "honeymoon" would go much more smoothly than the first two days, she was certain of that now. And in turn, she'd be able to put all her fantasizing aside and concentrate on what was important—her career at *Happily Ever After*.

As she walked, she distractedly rubbed the sore spot on her hip again, worried that it might stiffen up before she had a chance to return to the cabin and to a hot tub. Suddenly, she felt Mitch's hand replace hers. His warm palm softly massaged her backside. She snapped her gaze up in surprise.

"Why don't you let me rub that for you?" he said

with a wicked grin. "That's what husbands do, isn't it?"

Lianne groaned inwardly, then shook her head. Well, perhaps there were just a few more things they had to get straight.

MITCH SAT AT THE TABLE for four, listening to another one of Kip Albright's endless law school stories. They'd just finished their salads, and he hated to think that he'd be trapped at the table for at least another hour. Lianne had been right. Kip was a boor, a self-absorbed, egotistical boor.

He glanced over at the empty spot at the table, wishing that Lianne was sitting there. At least with her at his side, he'd have something pretty to look at while listening to Kip. But she'd decided to skip dinner that evening, preferring instead to nurse her bruised back at the cabin with room service and a long soak in the tub for two.

Mitch had offered to stay and have dinner with her, but she wasn't in much of a mood for conversation. She wanted solitude and was intent on having just that, nearly shoving him out the front door. Before he'd left, he'd even offered to let her have the bed again, hoping that might improve her mood. But she'd refused, determined to stick to the terms of their deal.

The damn deal. He was downright sick of it getting between them. He wasn't operating under any rules, like she was, but simply letting his impulses take their own course. He didn't put his arm around her because it looked good, he did it because he wanted to touch her, to feel her body beneath his fingers. And he didn't want to kiss her because it made him appear to be a better husband. He wanted to kiss her because he needed to feel her in his arms, to figure out if the desire he felt was something more than just simple lust.

Could it be more? He'd always been attracted to Lianne, but he never remembered being quite so obsessed. The sex in their marriage was good, but it had never come close to the nagging desire he'd been fighting these last few days.

He thought about her all the time, when they were together during the day, and especially when they were apart at night. As he lay in the heart-shaped bed, he'd listen for her breathing, for the little sighs she made when she slept. Then he'd close his eyes and try to conjure up the memory of her naked in bed beside him.

But the memory was always vague and unfocused, and he cursed himself for not recalling more vividly how her warm flesh felt against his body, how it felt to brace himself above her and lose himself inside her. He'd done all that before, but now he wanted to do it again, to really feel this time, instead of merely going through the motions.

He'd been such a fool to take all that for granted, thinking he'd have all the time in the world to love her. Five years was all he'd had before she walked out, and he'd done a damn poor job of it during that time.

Mitch picked up his knife and idly drew lazy patterns on the linen tablecloth, nodding every so often to satisfy Kip. At least old Kip had a rapt audience in his wife. Kelly Jean hadn't said more than a few words, except to laugh in the right places and encourage Kip to tell another long-winded tale.

He was almost relieved when Clarissa Bliss came hurrying up to the table, her ever-present clipboard clutched in her hands. "Hello, happy honeymooners!" she cried. Her gaze flitted to Mitch, and she put on a pout. "And one not-so-happy honeymooner. I heard about Lianne's problems on the trail this morning. Poor thing. I see she isn't here for dinner. Is she all right?"

"I think she'll be fine," Mitch said. "She's just tired."

Clarissa leaned closer. "Why don't you stop by my office after you're finished with dinner. We'll find a way to make it up to Lianne. I wouldn't want our reputation to suffer here at the Pocono Pines. Our motto is Every Honeymooner Is a Happy Honeymooner!"

Mitch tossed his napkin on the table and stood. "Actually, I'm really not hungry right now. And I'd like to check on Lianne. Why don't we talk on my way back to the cabin?"

He said his good-nights to a disappointed Kip and Kelly Jean, then followed Clarissa through the dining room and into the lobby. As soon as they were alone, she turned to him with a worried look. "I didn't want to say anything in front of the Albrights, but is everything all right between you and Lianne?"

Taken aback by her intense concern, Mitch quickly nodded. "Sure, everything is fine."

"Well, you have to trust me on these matters. I've been dealing with honeymooners for over twenty years and I can spot trouble when I see it. So I want to nip it right in the bud. You and Lianne deserve to have a perfect honeymoon."

"It's been good so far," Mitch offered.

She arched her eyebrow and gave him a disbelieving look. "Is it? You can tell Clarissa Bliss if you're having a problem. No one ever bothers to say how difficult the first few weeks of marriage are."

Mitch held up his hand. "Really, we're fine. No problems." Not if he didn't count the fact that all he could think about was dragging his "wife" off to bed, pulling her clothes off and making crazy love to her. But considering he and Lianne were no longer husband and wife, that didn't really count as a problem.

"Well, I know Lianne was upset during your trail ride today."

"How did you know that?"

"Our employees are trained to watch for the signs," she replied, giving him a sympathetic pat on the arm. "Don't be embarrassed, it happens to many couples. We'll just need to get you back on track." Clarissa whipped through the papers on her clipboard, then brightened. "We'll start with a wonderful breakfast in bed tomorrow morning. Very romantic, very sexy. And I see here that Lianne likes dancing."

"She does?"

Clarissa looked up at him in surprise. "You didn't know that?" She turned the clipboard toward him. "See, it's right here on her Happy Honeymooner profile."

"I guess we've just never gone dancing before," Mitch murmured.

"Well, that's going to change. After your breakfast in bed, I'm going to schedule Lianne for a wonderful treatment at our spa. Massage, manicure, pedicure, herbal wrap. How does eleven o'clock sound?"

Mitch shrugged. "I guess that would be all right."

"Then I'm going to schedule you both for a private dance lesson with Monsieur Maurice. Late tomorrow afternoon. Oh, it will be so romantic. Just the thing to put you both in the mood." She gave him a conspiratorial smile. "I guarantee, you'll be tangoing together in no time."

This time her meaning was completely clear. Somehow, Clarissa had found out that he and Lianne weren't sharing the same bed. Had they been so careless as to leave clues for the maid? If the riding instructor was reporting back to Clarissa, no doubt she had the maid checking in with her observations. Only one side of the heart-shaped bed had been slept in and the sofa looked well-used. Mitch could imagine what was going through her mind.

It was better Clarissa believed they were having troubles in the sack than suspect Lianne of being a reviewer from *Happily Ever After*. He could live with her interference. A slow smile curled his lips. In fact, if he played his cards right, Clarissa might just prove to be a big help.

"Is there anything else you'd suggest?" he asked.

"Well, no woman can resist a man in a dinner jacket and bow tie," she said. "We have formal wear rentals right here on the property." She handed him the clipboard. "Just write down your size and I can arrange for a tux to be delivered to the dance studio. And a single rose for Lianne. Won't she be surprised? Oh, I know this will all work out for the best. You just tell her to meet you at the studio after her day at the spa. I'll take care of everything else." With that Clarissa grabbed her clipboard and bustled off, satisfied that she'd put the Cooper marriage back in order.

"I'm sure you will," Mitch murmured.

He turned and headed out of the lobby, his step light as he walked back to the cabin in the waning sunshine. With a woman like Clarissa Bliss on his side, what could go wrong? He'd never been much of a romantic, but she seemed to know exactly what would make Lianne melt into his arms. Breakfast in bed, a day of pampering and ballroom dancing. None of the three would have ever occurred to him.

All right, he probably could have figured out the rose on his own, but the tux was well beyond his scope of imagination. Still, it all did have a certain flair that was sure to appeal to a hopeless romantic like Lianne. In a way, he was sorry he'd never tried something like this when they were married. It certainly wouldn't have taken much effort. Maybe he would have been able to save his marriage.

The cabin was quiet when he opened the front door. He glanced at the sofa, expecting to see Lianne asleep, or resting, from her ordeal on horseback. But the sofa was empty.

As he closed the door behind him, he heard a soft

bubbling sound from the rear of the cabin. He walked toward the whirlpool, surprised that Lianne had left it on, only to find her up to her neck in bubbles—and sound asleep.

Mitch chuckled softly. "Oh, the things you do to me," he said, his gaze taking in the shape of her perfect breasts just below the surface of the water. He fought the temptation to strip himself naked and join her, to pull her body against his and to savor the feel of her, with only the bubbles to come between them.

After they had played in the water for a while, he'd help her out of the tub. She'd be all flushed and ready for him, and he'd slowly possess her with his lips, first her mouth, then her breasts, and then every other inch of warm, moist flesh. And then, when she was hot for him, he'd take her, so slowly and so gently that it would all seem like a dream.

Mitch drew a sharp breath and dragged his gaze away from her naked body. A fine fantasy, but one that hadn't a chance of coming true. At least not yet. Lianne was still wary in his presence. If he climbed into the tub with her, she'd be out of the water like a shot.

No, if he wanted anything to happen between them, he would have to be careful, to proceed at a more leisurely pace, giving her the time to realize that they deserved a second chance.

Reluctantly, he turned away from the tub and walked back to the front door. With a great show of force, he yanked it open, then slammed it shut. He clomped around in the recesses of the sitting room, called her name once or twice, then heard a frantic splashing.

"Just a minute!" she cried. "Stay right there! I'll be right out."

Mitch leaned back against the door and crossed his arms over his chest, waiting for his "wife" to appear. She did, a few moments later, wrapped securely in her robe, damp tendrils of hair sticking to her neck and temples.

He winced as he watched her limp toward him. God, she looked like she was in pain, her jaw tight, her forehead creased. "Are you all right?"

"I'm fine," she murmured. "Except for the bruise on my butt the size of Montana. I sat in the hot tub, and that seemed to help a little bit. I just need to get some sleep." She moved toward the sofa, grabbing her blanket and pillow along the way, but Mitch intercepted her.

He tossed the pillow and blanket on the floor, then swung her up into his arms. She gave a little screech, then frantically tried to rearrange her robe to hide the tantalizing sights beneath the terry cloth. "Ow! Mitch, stop! What are you doing?"

"This will only hurt for a minute," he said, heading for the stairs.

Her eyes went wide and she started to sputter. "Wh—where are you taking me? Mitch, stop this instant. I am not going to—"

"Annie, just keep quiet. I know what's good for you."

Her breath caught, and she blinked hard as he took

the steps two at a time. "Mitch, I don't think that this is the time or the—"

Without an ounce of ceremony, or sympathy, he dropped her onto the heart-shaped bed. She lay there, rendered speechless, the robe slipping off her shoulders, her chest heaving. He stood over her and watched her for a long moment, once again fighting an overwhelming urge, this time to join her in bed. After all, she fully expected him to, and maybe she'd even welcome the attempt.

But he'd decided to take things slowly. He wasn't about to mess up what might be his one and only chance at making Lianne love him again. Because that's all he would settle for, not just a night or two of feverish sex, but something deeper. He wanted his wife back, and damned if he wasn't going to do his best to make that happen.

"Go to sleep, Lianne. You'll be much more comfortable here in bed. I'll take the sofa."

With that, he turned and started down the stairs. He heard her gasp in surprise, then scramble out of the bed. He could feel her eyes on him as he descended to the sitting room. And he heard the soft pad of her footsteps as she walked to the loft railing and peeked over.

Mitch smiled to himself. Patience. That's what it was all about. Hell, anything worth having was worth waiting for, wasn't it?

SHE WOKE UP SLOWLY, deliciously, stretching sinuously beneath satiny sheets. All the little aches and pains of the day before had dulled. Lianne opened her eyes to the sunlight streaming through the windows. For a moment, she wasn't sure where she was. But then she remembered Mitch putting her into his bed last night and leaving her there—alone.

Hesitantly, she lifted the sheet, just to make certain nothing had happened in the middle of the night that she'd missed. But she was still dressed in his faded T-shirt, the one she'd pulled from his duffel bag after he dumped her into bed. A small sliver of disappointment shot through her.

She was almost hoping that he'd snuck upstairs in the dark of night, crawled into bed with her and ravished her. She could use a good ravishing right about now, especially after sleeping in such close proximity to him for the past two nights. It had been more than a few months since she'd even been in the same room with a man she found sexually attractive. She hadn't dated much since the divorce was final, and the few relationships she'd had that got as far as the bedroom had ended shortly thereafter.

It wasn't that she didn't want a healthy relationship with good, or maybe even great, sex. It's just that all the pain of losing Mitch, watching their marriage disintegrate before her eyes, was too much to bear a second time. She'd gone through that once, and she never wanted to go through it again.

So why couldn't she seem to think of anything else but starting it all up once more with Mitch? They failed the first time around—what made her think they'd do any better given a second chance? Lianne sighed and stared up at the ceiling.

Perhaps because they had changed? She'd grown up a whole lot these past five years, and Mitch certainly wasn't anything like the man she'd married. They were both different people, in different places in their lives.

She sat up in bed and impatiently brushed the sleep out of her eyes. It would do no good to think about things that could never be! This was strictly a business arrangement, one that lent itself to a few wayward daydreams, but still a business arrangement. After their "honeymoon" was over, they'd go their separate ways, only to do the same thing all over again a few months later. There was nothing happening to indicate that Mitch was interested in a lasting relationship.

"Hey, sleepyhead, are you awake?"

Lianne rubbed her eyes again, then watched Mitch come up the stairs, balancing a tray in his arms. To her surprise, a bellhop followed him with a silver bucket and two champagne glasses. She pulled the sheets up around her chin and watched them both as they arranged things on the chest at the foot of the bed.

"What's this?" she asked.

Mitch grinned. "For my lovely wife. Breakfast in bed. With champagne."

The bellhop nimbly popped the cork on the champagne, then made a quick exit down the stairs. She glanced up at Mitch and smiled hesitantly. "Did you do this?"

"I had some help." He grabbed the bottle of champagne and the glasses and sat down beside her on the bed. He wore only a pair of baggy sweatpants, the gathered waist making his hips look even leaner than they were. His chest was bare with only a light sprinkling of hair across the smooth skin. She wanted to reach out and touch him, but instead she watched him fill the glasses, clenching her hands at her sides. He handed her a flute filled with fizzing bubbles and pale wine.

"I don't think I've ever had champagne for breakfast. This is a real treat."

He tipped his glass toward hers. "This day is going to be full of surprises," he murmured. Their glasses touched, and the crystal made a clear and perfect sound. "To us," he said.

She blinked, not sure what to reply. After all, the bellhop was well out of earshot. "To us," she finally said.

Mitch took a sip of his champagne, then got up and retrieved the tray from the end of the bed. He deftly pulled the silver covers off the dishes, then set the tray next to her. "Hungry?"

She nodded. "I—I feel a lot better today. I was afraid I was going to be sore from the ride yesterday, but I think it helped to get a good night's sleep. The bed was heaven. That sofa is really lumpy."

His gaze flicked up to hers. "I know, I've experienced it firsthand."

"I didn't want to take your bed."

"I wanted you in my bed," he replied softly.

Uneasy with his odd mood, she reached out and snatched up a piece of bacon from the plate. She studied him covertly as she munched on it. But he seemed intent on buttering a piece of toast, then slathering it with jam.

When he was finished, he held it out in front of her mouth. "Have a taste," he murmured.

She bent forward and took a bite, her gaze locked with his. The toast felt like sandpaper in her mouth, and she swallowed it without chewing. What *was* this game he was playing with her now? This sexy, tantalizing way he had about him this morning.

"So you aren't sore this morning?"

She shook her head.

"That's good." The corners of his mouth turned up in a slight smile. He picked up a fork and cut into a cheese omelet, then speared the piece and held it out to her. "Try this."

She did as she was told, and over the next few minutes he gave her a taste of everything on the tray. Lianne frowned. If she didn't know better, she'd suspect his behavior was part of a grand plan to get back into her good graces. Mitch Cooper wanted something, only she wasn't quite sure what it was.

"This is really all very nice," she commented. "You decided to do this all on your own?"

"In a manner of speaking," he replied.

"Why?" she asked, deciding to take a direct approach.

Mitch chuckled. "What do you mean? Do I have to have a reason to treat my wife to breakfast in bed?"

"I'm not your wife," she reminded him.

"Do I have to have a reason to treat my *ex*-wife to

breakfast in bed?" he amended. "Just enjoy it. We're supposed to be on our honeymoon."

"I'm not going rock climbing."

"I canceled that," he replied. "I thought we'd find something else to do with our time."

"Like what?"

"Oh, we'll just see what comes along." He glanced up, and when their eyes met, she shivered. "I'd like to keep my options open."

Her gaze fell to his mouth, to his perfectly sculpted lips. "Are—are you planning to collect on our bet? Is that what this is about?"

"Our bet?"

"You know, the kiss." She looked up at him through her lashes.

"Ah, the kiss. I'd forgotten all about that." He considered the subject for a moment, then shook his head. "I think I'll save that for later. You don't mind, do you?"

She shook her head.

"Good." He stood up and glanced at his watch. "Then, finish up your breakfast. It's ten-thirty and you're due at the spa at eleven."

She watched him suspiciously. "What did you sign us up for now? I thought we agreed that—"

"You'll like this," he said, bending toward her to smooth his hand idly over her hair. "I guarantee it. Now, hurry up or you'll be late. Your clothes and things are in the dresser. I brought them up from downstairs early this morning."

She opened her mouth to **protest**, then snapped it

shut when he turned and walked back downstairs. Slowly, she leaned against the headboard of the bed, frowning. Yesterday, she'd been a resident of the sofa, and this morning she was installed quite comfortably in his bed. What exactly did this mean?

Would he be sleeping on the sofa? Or did he expect to join her in the bed sometime in the near future? A tiny shudder of anticipation set her hands trembling, and she clutched them in front of her.

Everything was happening so fast, racing toward an inevitable conclusion in this very bed. She knew she should stop it right now, that what they were moving toward was pure folly. But she didn't want to stop.

She wanted Mitch in this bed, with her. And she wasn't about to do anything to keep that from happening.

5

"No, NO, NO! That eez not it! You must hold her like you want to make mad, passionate love to her! Put your bodies together." Monsieur Maurice placed a hand on Lianne's back, then on Mitch's, and pressed them toward each other until Lianne's hips were planted squarely against her ex-husband's.

A flood of warmth seeped into her cheeks, and for a moment she had trouble catching a breath. She felt every contour of his body through the thin fabric of her sundress, and for all she could tell, everything was exactly where she remembered it to be.

The little mustachioed man stepped back and observed them critically, his thumb tucked under his chin and his finger tapping his cheek. Then he scurried around them, adjusting a hand here and a shoulder there, until he was satisfied. "There, that eez much better, *n'est-ce pas?* We do not hold our *cherie* like a sack of potatoes!"

"It's good for me," Mitch murmured in her ear. "Is it good for you?"

She glanced up at him, then flicked her gaze away as another unbidden shiver raced through her. She'd been sneaking glances at her ex-husband since she arrived at the dance studio, fresh and relaxed from her afternoon at the spa.

Where he found the white dinner jacket, she had no idea, but he looked so incredibly dashing, so handsome, that when he presented her with a single rose, she nearly melted into a puddle at his feet. She now held the rose clutched in her white-knuckled hand and watched it bounce over Mitch's shoulder as they both perfected the steps of a simple tango.

The entire day had been one surprise after another. First a champagne breakfast in bed, then a complete afternoon of pampering. When her manicurist gave her a note from Mitch telling her to meet him at the dance studio, she wasn't sure what to think. But she'd never expected anything like this. Except for the obligatory waltzes at their wedding, Mitch Cooper had never shown the slightest interest in dancing. And now, here he was, dressed like some romantic movie hero, trying his best to keep from stepping on her toes.

The truth be told, he was doing quite well. He always was the more coordinated one. It was Lianne who kept fumbling around. Every time their bodies brushed against each other, she nearly jumped out of her skin, her very smooth and sloughed skin. But Mitch seemed cool and composed, as if all this bodily contact didn't bother him in the least.

As Monsieur Maurice had taken them through the waltz, then the cha-cha and finally the tango, she'd kept her mind occupied with the events of the day. But no matter how many times she reasoned through it all, she just couldn't figure out what Mitch was up to. He seemed so concerned for her comfort and happiness, so anxious to please her.

Lianne could feel her palm sweating in his hand, and she couldn't help but wonder when he'd notice. She groaned inwardly. It took all her willpower to simply move her feet with the music and keep her eyes fixed on something other than Mitch's face. She had no energy to worry about her sweaty palms.

"Relax," Mitch said, bending to whisper in her ear. She held her breath as he nuzzled her hair. "This is supposed to be fun. You feel like you're ready to sit down for a ten-hour root canal."

"I—I just feel a little clumsy," she said.

He let his hand slide down to the small of her back. "You don't feel that way to me. You feel...good. Very good."

Monsieur Maurice clapped his hands softly. "Ah, zees eez much better. We are feeling like lovers again. But we must look into each other's eyes. Zees is part of the tango. Come, come. You must try! I know you can do eet! After all, you have Monsieur Maurice for zee teacher. He is zee best!"

Lianne pulled back slightly and risked a glance up at Mitch. When their gazes locked, her breath stopped in her throat. His eyes were dark with unconcealed desire, more desire than Monsieur Maurice had called for. She blinked, but she wasn't able to break the connection between them. A nearly imperceptible smile curved the corners of his lips, and Lianne felt as if she were sinking to the bottom of a deep, dark pool.

"Oh, I like zees look!" Monsieur Maurice cried. "Oh,

zee passion, zee raw animal magnetism. We are cooking now, *n'est-ce pas?*"

"I am feeling a little warm," Mitch said with a lazy grin. "How about you?"

"Maybe we should take a break?" Lianne's voice cracked, and she cleared her throat to cover her nerves.

Mitch smoothly turned her, following the steps of the dance while all the while keeping her body molded against his. "I think we better keep dancing. Practice makes perfect."

"And what are we practicing for?"

He slid his hand up her back and wove his fingers through the hair at her nape. "For no reason except that I'm enjoying the feel of you in my arms again." He bent closer, his lips just inches from hers, and she could feel his warm breath like a caress on her cheek.

She tried to speak, but the words got caught somewhere in her throat. All she could manage was a strangled "Oh!" before she decided to keep her mouth shut.

The tango suddenly came to an end, and she and Mitch stopped dancing. "All right," Monsieur Maurice said, clapping his hands. "I think we have had enough of zees!"

Lianne turned to him and frowned. "You mean we're done? Already?"

"Oh, no, no, no, no! Now I will put on some music and leave you so you may dance among yourselves. Monsieur Maurice has done all he can!" With a flourish of his hand, he bowed to Lianne and nodded to Mitch, then gracefully exited the studio with an impossibly straight spine and out-turned toes.

When the door closed behind him, Lianne let out a long sigh. For a moment, the studio was silent and she was afraid to look at Mitch. But then another song started over the sound system and he drew her closer and began to move with the music. A dreamy version of "Isn't It Romantic" filled the empty studio, and she stumbled a bit before she got in step with Mitch.

"Are you having fun?" he asked.

She wasn't quite sure what she was having was called *fun*. An attack of the jitters was more like it. She felt like one of those eighteenth-century virgins on her wedding night, not quite sure what was going to happen next but more than a little curious. Curiosity mixed with a liberal dose of apprehension. "Sure," she said. "I'm having a lot of fun."

"I was surprised to find out that you like to dance. I never knew that about you."

"How did you find out?"

"Miss Bliss mentioned it in passing. You put it on your profile."

"Ah. I—I guess I did." She nodded, letting her response trail off.

"I suppose there are a lot of things I don't know about you. It's a little bit strange, considering that we were married for five years."

"We were different people back then," she said softly, tracing her finger along the shoulder of his jacket. "We were a lot younger."

"So you regret marrying me?"

"There's no use in regretting what happened. It just

happened, and there's not much we can do about it now."

"Isn't there?"

She shook her head and distractedly plucked at the loose thread on the lapel of his jacket. "Mitch, I'm not going to rehash all the things that went wrong in our marriage. Believe me, I've done that more times than I care to count. And I never seem to come up with any answers. It just didn't work, that's all."

"So we should just forget it."

She nodded.

"Put it in the past," he added.

She glanced up at him and nodded again.

"And start fresh."

His words took a moment to register, but when they did she swallowed hard, her heart jolting in her chest. "I—I don't understand."

"It's simple, really. All we have to do is forget the past. Put it all behind us. For the rest of this week, let's just pretend that we don't have a past together."

"Just like that? Forget it all?"

"Everyone else here is just beginning their lives together. We're the only couple who has finished ours. Maybe we should try it their way. Look forward to all the possibilities instead of looking back."

"I guess that would help," she said. "I—I mean, in my attitude, and in my evaluation of this resort. It would help if I looked at it from that perspective, like a real honeymooner."

His eyebrow arched. "And maybe you should forget

about our little deal. Just put that in the back of your mind, too. All in the name of objectivity, of course."

"All right. I suppose I could do that."

Mitch grinned and pulled her closer. "Good. Now, let's quit talking and dance."

As they moved to the music, Lianne relaxed in his arms. He talked to her softly as they danced, telling silly stories, teasing her, humming along with the tune. One song ran into another, and time seemed to spin out around them, the studio growing dim in the late afternoon light.

His hands, warm and firm, skimmed across her body, and she closed her eyes and lost herself in his touch. How long had it been since she'd been touched like this? Had she *ever* been touched like this? When every movement of his fingers left a trail of humming anticipation? When every sensation left her longing for more?

She wanted him to kiss her, but she wasn't sure how to go about it. Should she tip her face up to his and close her eyes? Or should she trace the shape of his mouth with her fingers? There had to be a way to take that next step.

"What are you thinking?" he murmured. "Tell me."

Lianne smiled, embarrassed. "I can't."

"Yes, you can. Don't be afraid, Annie. Tell me."

"I—I was thinking that I wanted you to kiss me," she said, her voice breathy, her heart pounding. "I wanted to settle our wager—once and for all."

He sighed and tipped his head back, smiling ruefully. "I can't kiss you, Annie," he said, his admission sending a surge of disappointment through her.

"Why not?"

"Because if I kiss you now, I won't be able to stop. I'll want to kiss you all evening and right into the night."

She shrugged in an attempt at nonchalance, but her heart thudded so hard that she could barely hear her own words. "That would be all right with me."

He stopped dancing and stepped away from her, but his gaze stayed locked on hers, his eyes dark in the dim light. "Then, let's get out of here," he said, holding out his hand.

Stilling a tremble in her fingers, she reached for him, knowing full well that if she walked out that door with him, she might come to regret it. Perhaps not tonight, or tomorrow, but probably and very likely in the near future.

But that didn't stop her from grasping his hand and making her way toward the door of the studio. For she knew that if she didn't go with Mitch, there would be other regrets, ones that might plague her for the rest of her life.

THEY STROLLED ALONG the path toward the cabin, her hand clasped in his. Mitch could see her sneaking a sideways glance every few steps and wondered what was running through her mind. Was she frightened of him, or was she merely anticipating what might happen between them?

There would be a kiss, but would there be more?

It was time to force the issue, time to find out how

she really felt, beyond this deal and beyond this honeymoon. He knew what he wanted, and if that led to something deeper between them, then he was ready.

As they got closer to their cabin, she slowed a bit, her steps faltering. But Mitch held tight to her hand and pulled her along, down the path and up the front steps of the cabin and through the door, slamming it behind him.

In one quick movement, he yanked her into his arms and pinned her against the door, bringing his mouth down on hers. He molded his body against hers until he could feel her breasts through his shirt and her hips pressed to his. Then he proceeded to very thoroughly ravage her mouth.

She went soft in his arms, became pliant beneath his body, but he was careful not to break their intimate contact for fear that she might consider the kiss finished. An end was not what he had in mind. Instead, he wanted to taste her, to explore her mouth, until she was ready for him to move on to more intimate pleasures.

At first he felt her resist, stiffen beneath him, but he softened the kiss, until fire had turned to languid heat. His tongue teased hers, challenging her to give him more, promising untold pleasure if she did.

Finally, just when he thought she would draw away, she moaned softly and wrapped her arms around his neck, drawing him even closer. His blood surged, racing from his head to his groin, and he felt himself grow hard with need. He never expected to want her this much, or to be forced to slake his desire with just a kiss.

NO COST! NO OBLIGATION TO BUY! NO PURCHASE NECESSARY!

PLAY "LUCKY 7" AND GET FIVE FREE GIFTS

HOW TO PLAY:

1. With a coin, carefully scratch off the silver box at the right. Then check the claim chart to see what we have for you—FREE BOOKS and a gift—ALL YOURS! ALL FREE!

2. Send back this card and you'll receive brand-new Harlequin Temptation® novels. These books have a cover price of $3.50 each, but they are yours to keep absolutely free.

3. There's no catch. You're under no obligation to buy anything. We charge nothing—ZERO—for your first shipment. And you don't have to make any minimum number of purchases—not even one!

4. The fact is thousands of readers enjoy receiving books by mail from the Harlequin Reader Service®. They like the convenience of home delivery...they like getting the best new novels BEFORE they're available in stores...and they love our discount prices!

5. We hope that after receiving your free books you'll want to remain a subscriber. But the choice is yours—to continue or cancel, anytime at all! So why not take us up on our invitation, with no risk of any kind. You'll be glad you did!

You'll love this plush, cuddly Teddy Bear, an adorable accessory for your dressing table, bookcase or desk. Measuring 5½" tall, he's soft and brown and has a bright red ribbon around his neck—he's completely captivating! And he's yours absolutely free, when you accept this no-risk offer!

PLAY "LUCKY 7"

**Just scratch off the silver box with a coin.
Then check below to see the gifts you get.**

YES! I have scratched off the silver box. Please send me all the gifts for which I qualify. I understand I am under no obligation to purchase any books, as explained on the back and on the opposite page.

142 CIH A7C6
(U-H-T-03/97)

NAME _____

ADDRESS _____ APT. _____

CITY _____ STATE ____ ZIP ____

 WORTH FOUR FREE BOOKS PLUS A FREE CUDDLY TEDDY BEAR

 WORTH THREE FREE BOOKS

 WORTH TWO FREE BOOKS

WORTH ONE FREE BOOK

Offer limited to one per household and not valid to current Harlequin Temptation® subscribers. All orders subject to approval.

© 1990 HARLEQUIN ENTERPRISES LIMITED

PRINTED IN U.S.A.

THE HARLEQUIN READER SERVICE®: HERE'S HOW IT WORKS

Accepting free books places you under no obligation to buy anything. You may keep the books and gift and return the shipping statement marked "cancel". If you do not cancel, about a month later we'll send you 4 additional novels, and bill you just $2.90 each plus 25¢ delivery per book and applicable sales tax, if any.* That's the complete price—and compared to cover prices of $3.50 each—quite a bargain! You may cancel at any time, but if you choose to continue, every month we'll send you 4 more books, which you may either purchase at the discount price…or return to us and cancel your subscription.

*Terms and prices subject to change without notice. Sales tax applicable in N.Y.

BUSINESS REPLY MAIL
FIRST-CLASS MAIL   PERMIT NO. 717   BUFFALO, NY

POSTAGE WILL BE PAID BY ADDRESSEE

HARLEQUIN READER SERVICE
3010 WALDEN AVE
PO BOX 1867
BUFFALO NY 14240-9952

NO POSTAGE
NECESSARY
IF MAILED
IN THE
UNITED STATES

But he could go only as far as she allowed him, and he wasn't sure how far that might be.

He pulled back slightly, his lips still touching hers. "Tell me it's all right to stop and take a breath," he murmured.

"No," she replied, twisting her fingers through his hair. "I don't want you to stop. I like the way you kiss."

Mitch groaned as he savaged her mouth again, cupping her face in his hands, probing deeper until he knew it would never be deep enough. Breathing hard, he traced a line from her mouth to the base of her neck while he worked on the top buttons of her dress.

She cried out as he bit her softly, then moved up to the silken skin beneath her ear. "I can't get enough of you," he breathed. "I want more, Annie. Let me have more."

In answer, she dropped her hands from his neck and slowly began to unbutton the front of her dress. When she fumbled with the buttons, he pushed her hands away and finished the task himself. Parting the soft fabric, his hands slid up her rib cage until they cradled her breasts. She wriggled beneath him, and when she adjusted her hips against his, he felt himself step dangerously close to the edge.

Damn, he was no better than a horny teenager, hot and hard and ready to come. He drew a deep breath, and his body shuddered as he slowly regained control. His head cleared, his pulse slowed, and he allowed himself the time to tease at her hard-pebbled nipples through the silky fabric of her bra.

"Do you have any idea what you do to me?"

She met his gaze and mutely shook her head.

With a wicked smile, he grabbed her thigh and pulled her leg up along his hip. "This is what you do to me," he murmured, pressing his arousal hard against her. "This is what you've been doing to me since the day you showed up on my front porch."

"Mitch, I—"

He kissed her again, stopping her before she could go on. He knew what she was going to say, and he didn't want to hear it. He didn't want to hear that this might be a mistake, that they better slow down before they both did something they'd be sorry for later.

To hell with all the analysis and the doubts. He was existing on pure, raw emotion. He didn't want to use his head, he just wanted to keep feeling until he'd spent every ounce of his desire for her. He wanted to show her what it could have been like between them, had he known better.

He was older now, and wiser. Wise enough to real-ize that the sensations raging through his mind and body were like nothing he'd ever felt with a woman be-fore, not even when he'd been married to Lianne.

All the pieces had been there, but he'd been too stu-pid to figure out how to put them together. How to al-low himself to want her, how to make her want him be-yond all comprehension. They'd been just two kids playing at true love, neither one knowing that they hadn't even scratched the surface.

"Don't think, Annie," he whispered, his voice hoarse with passion, his hands frantically stripping her dress from her shoulders. "Just feel. Feel what we are together. Have you ever felt this way before?"

She shook her head, letting the dress slip to her waist, then setting to work on the buttons of his pleated shirt. Impatient, she tugged at the bow tie, then threw it over his shoulder. His shirt fell open and she stopped, staring at his chest, her hands just inches from his skin.

"Touch me, sweetheart. I want your hands on me."

Slowly, exquisitely, she splayed her fingers across his chest, smoothing her cool palms over the contours, pushing his shirt apart along the way. He sucked in a sharp breath as her nails skimmed his nipples, drawing in the sweet fragrance of her hair until it filled his head.

She bent and pressed her forehead against his heart. "I—I don't believe this is happening. Where did all this come from?"

Mitch growled playfully and nuzzled his face in the curve of her neck. "You can thank Clarissa Bliss. She gave me some good advice."

Lianne pushed back, her palms firm against his chest. "What?"

"Miss Bliss. She suggested all of this. She thought our marriage was in trouble, that we were having problems, so she took me aside last night after dinner and gave me a few helpful hints."

She scowled. "Clarissa Bliss helped you plan this— this seduction?"

Mitch smiled, ready to agree, then frowned. "Well, I

wouldn't put it that way. She just steered me in the right direction."

Lianne's expression hardened. "The breakfast in bed, that was your idea?"

"No, not exactly."

"And the afternoon at the spa and the dance lessons?"

"No. But I—"

"The rose?" she demanded. "Tell me at least *that* was your idea."

He opened his mouth to reply, but decided that it would probably be better not to answer at all. The look in her eyes was enough to wither any further attempt at an explanation. And to douse his raging desire, as well. "What difference does it make who thought of it, Annie? It all served its purpose, didn't it?"

"Served its purpose?" she shouted. "Served its purpose! Of all the underhanded, manipulative, slimy—"

"Wait." He covered her mouth with his hand, but she jerked away. "That didn't come out the way I meant it. I just meant to say that it doesn't matter how we got here. Just that we got here."

He reached for her and she took a step back. "Don't you dare touch me." Muttering beneath her breath, she scrambled to pull her dress over her arms, shoving her trembling hands through the sleeves and buttoning each button while offering vivid denunciations of his character.

"What is the damn difference?" he asked.

"If you don't know, then I'm not going to take the time to tell you."

"I don't know. Annie, you've got to believe me, I didn't mean to upset you. I thought this would make you happy."

"No, Mitch, you thought it would make *you* happy. You thought if you turned on the charm, that I'd forget everything that's passed between us. Well, I fell for your manipulations once and I married you. I'm not going to be stupid enough to fall for you again."

"Lianne, I was not—"

She held up her hand. "Just save it, because I don't want to hear it." With that she flung open the door and strode out. He watched her hurry down the path, her fists clenched at her sides, her tousled hair flying around her face.

Cursing softly, he shut the door and leaned back against it, then ran his fingers through his hair. Hell, for a guy who thought he had finally figured out what made Annie Cooper tick, he'd sure managed to overwind her springs.

He shook his head and sighed. So what if he'd messed up. He'd just have to make sure he got another chance. If she didn't want to give him one, he'd simply take it. And another and another, if he needed them. But sooner or later, he was going to get this thing right between him and Annie.

Sooner or later, she'd fall in love with him again.

"MEN ARE PIGS."

Kelly Jean straightened on her bar stool and held up her half-empty margarita. "They're lower than pigs," she said, her words slurred. "They're...pig's feet." She hiccuped once, then took another swig of her drink.

Lianne had found Kelly Jean weeping into her tequila when she walked in the bar. At first, she hesitated, not wanting to get sucked into another conversation with the terminally perky newlywed. But the girl looked so forlorn, so absolutely miserable, that she couldn't let her sit alone, drowning her sorrows. And she had to find out what Kip had done to throw his adoring wife into such a state. So she sat down beside her and ordered a gin and tonic.

"Do you know what he said to me?" Kelly Jean asked for the third time.

Lianne smiled, snatching her glass up before Kelly Jean knocked it over. "You told me already."

"He said that he didn't marry me for my brains. Can you believe that? How could he say something so nasty? I thought he loved me."

Her eyes filled with fresh tears, and Lianne reached out and patted her hand sympathetically. Kelly Jean grabbed a bar napkin and blew her nose. "I mean, I know I'm not as smart as he is. But he always wants to be the one who knows everything. I thought that made him happy. So I just went along. I'm not that dumb, you know. I could have passed every one of my classes in college, maybe even gotten a B if I had wanted to. It's—it's just that they didn't seem very important at the time. Not after I knew I was going to marry my Kippy."

"Maybe you should have thought about what you wanted," Lianne suggested.

She sniffled. "Darn tootin'. From now on, *I'm* number one." She jabbed a thumb to her chest with such enthusiasm, she nearly knocked herself off her bar stool.

Lianne reached out to steady her. "I think you should tell Kip how you feel."

Kelly Jean's eyes went wide. "I couldn't do that."

"Why not?"

"Because he never listens when I try to talk about us. He thinks that we shouldn't have to talk about our relationship. As far as he's concerned, everything is just hunky-dory." She threw out her hands, nearly hitting Lianne in the face. "Well, I'm saying it's not. In fact, I'm saying our relationship stinks like a month-old salmon steak."

"That bad, huh."

"Like the one that was left in the trunk of Kip's BMW," she added. "One that I forgot to take out after I went grocery shopping for his mother. Boy, was he ticked off. His precious car, all smelly." She giggled. "I thought it was kind of funny."

"So what are you going to do?" Lianne asked. "You can't go on like this."

"Maybe I should tell him he's a pig and let him figure out what to do."

A redhead sitting a few stools away leaned over and looked at them both. "I thought our honeymoon would be perfect," she said woefully. "We had a fight this morning about my mother and he decided to go golfing, all by himself. He's golfed thirty-six holes so far today, and he doesn't show any signs of wanting to stop."

"Men are pigs," Kelly Jean repeated.

"I second that," the redhead said, sliding over a few stools. "I'm Emily Saunders." She held out her hand, and both Kelly Jean and Lianne shook it as they introduced themselves.

"Lianne says we should speak up," Kelly Jean commented.

"Experience tells me that if you let these types of things fester, it will only harm your marriage."

"What experience?" Emily asked.

Kelly Jean turned her attention to Lianne. "Yeah, what experience? Aren't you in the same boat as we are, drowning your problems in drink while your new husband is off doing heaven knows what?"

"I have some experience," Lianne countered. "In fact, I've been married before."

Kelly Jean's jaw dropped. "You have? You mean Mitch is your second husband?"

"In a manner of speaking," Lianne said. "Don't act so surprised. There are a lot of women who marry twice, sometimes even three times. In my first marriage I had the same problems you're having. I was a wimp. I didn't speak up for what I wanted. And I found myself just disappearing. I wasn't Lianne anymore, I was someone's wife. So this time around, I decided I'd get it right. I don't let Mitch call all the shots. In fact, I don't let him call many of the shots. And I'm much happier now."

Kelly Jean nodded, an intense expression on her flushed face. "So we should just lay down the law to our husbands right now?"

"There's no better time," Lianne said. "If you don't get things straight from the start, there's bound to be problems later. Just explain exactly what's acceptable to you, and if he refuses, tell him to take a flying leap."

"You mean I should tell Kip to quit making jokes about my IQ?" Kelly Jean asked.

"And I should demand that Eddie talk nice about my mother?" Emily asked.

Lianne nodded. "Tell them now, before they get too set in their ways."

The two of them stood up at the same time and pushed away from the bar. "I hope this works," Kelly Jean said.

"Me, too," Emily said.

They linked arms and wobbled out. Lianne turned back to her drink and smiled. Now that she had the Albright and Saunders marriages on the right path, what was she going to do about hers? Not her marriage, actually, but everything that was going on between her and Mitch.

When she'd set out on this plan to pose as honeymooners, she thought it would be so easy. She and Mitch had remained on amicable terms, he had a flexible job and needed a vacation, and she had absolutely no intentions of revisiting their marriage.

But they weren't really revisiting their marriage, were they? All that had passed over the last few days—the last few hours, to be precise—didn't have a whole lot to do with their marriage. Except that perhaps the pace of events was somewhat faster due to the fact that she and Mitch had spent time in bed in the past.

Still, she couldn't help but draw parallels between Mitch's behavior now and Mitch's behavior back then. He'd always had a single-minded purpose about him. When he wanted something, he went after it and didn't let up until he got it. He had wanted a wife, Lianne to be precise. He'd wooed her and won her, then moved on to his next goal in life, never once expending any energy to keep her.

Was that what he was up to now? Was seduction suddenly a priority? And once he'd managed to seduce her, what then? Would he leave her and move on to something—or someone—even more challenging?

She couldn't go through this again, to fall in love with him a second time and then lose him. They'd done it all once before and failed. What made her think anything had changed?

Lianne idly twirled the swizzle stick in her drink, staring at the ice cubes as they clinked against the side of the glass. She had changed. And Mitch had, too, or at least he seemed to have made some major alterations in his life. He no longer had the job that had kept them apart. And maybe with the job, he'd lost a bit of that all-consuming drive that had turned her into an outsider in her own marriage. He seemed much easier with the person she was now than he had been when they'd been married.

And he wanted her, that much was clear. During their marriage, she had never sensed much passion in him. They had made love, but it was never as wild and frantic and breathlessly desperate as it had been with them earlier tonight. He'd made her forget all her resolve, all her good sense. He'd made her want him with a desire she couldn't control.

And in all that, he'd also frightened her. She was afraid to let go, afraid to open her heart and soul to him again. So she'd taken the first out she could get, and it had come in the form of Clarissa Bliss. Was she really angry that he'd taken her advice? After all, Clarissa hadn't been standing behind him, mouthing all the wonderful things he'd said to her throughout the day. Clarissa hadn't been there to tell him how to touch her heart, how to look into her eyes in that irresistible, sexy way he had, how to make her burn with passion.

Lianne took a long sip of her drink. She wanted Mitch as much as he wanted her. But she didn't want a replay of what they'd had before. She pinched her eyes shut.

So she was a grown woman, wasn't she? If she wanted to have a passionate affair with her ex-husband, what was stopping her? As long as she was in control, she couldn't get hurt, right? And there didn't have to be any expectations, beyond having a good time in bed. Without expectations, she had nothing to fear.

She could do this! She could keep everything she'd worked for in her life and have Mitch as well—on her own terms. She'd call the shots, she'd decide when it was over. And she wouldn't let herself love him again. It was as simple as that.

As Lianne gulped down the last of her watery drink, she attempted to formulate a plan. Now that she'd decided exactly what she wanted, she'd have to figure out how she was going to get Mitch to seduce her again. She hadn't done much the last time around to encourage further attempts. In fact, she wouldn't be surprised if Mitch steered a clear path around her for the rest of the week.

There would be only one way. If she wanted Mitch, she'd have to take matters into her own hands. She'd have to seduce him!

Determined to put her plan into action, Lianne slipped off the bar stool and turned for the door. But she'd barely taken a step before Clarissa Bliss rushed up to her, her usually perfect coif now in complete disarray. She placed her hands on the bar and seemed to waver a bit, then motioned to the bartender. "Give me a daiquiri. No, wait, make that a vodka martini. A double." The bartender turned, but at the last moment, she grabbed him by the sleeve. "Forget the martini, I'll take a boilermaker, with a double shot of whiskey."

The bartender fetched her drink and she downed the whiskey in two quick gulps than delicately sipped at her beer. It was then, over the rim of the mug, that she noticed Lianne. At first she seemed surprised, but then a desperate look crossed her features.

"You're probably wondering what I'm doing in here."

Lianne shook her head.

"You would not believe what has just happened. In fact, maybe you would, since you know the Albrights. It seems our sweet little Kelly Jean got it into her head to confront her husband over some little tiff they had." Clarissa waved her hand impatiently. "Don't ask me what it was about. She stood out on the dock and yelled at him until he rowed in from the middle of the lake. There was a big fight, she slapped his face with a fish and pushed him in the water. And now he's talking divorce and she's talking divorce." Clarissa moaned. "And if that isn't bad enough, the Saunderses just had a huge blowup in the lobby while they were waiting to be seated for dinner. And their dinner partners, the Conroys, took sides, and now they're all mad at each other."

Lianne shifted nervously. "Well, these things happen, don't they?"

"Not to Clarissa Bliss! And not at the Pocono Pines Honeymoon Resort! We pride ourselves in giving all our couples a perfect honeymoon. And now this. This could ruin our reputation. I could lose my job. Do you have any idea how serious this is?"

"I—I guess not. But surely everything will work itself out, if you just give it time."

Clarissa moaned and laid her head on the bar. "I don't have time. Rumor has it that there's a reviewer on the way from *Happily Ever After* magazine. He—or she—might even be here as we speak, watching this place go up in flames."

A smile quirked the corners of Lianne's mouth, and she fought back the impulse to laugh. What would Miss Bliss have to say if she learned the reviewer from *Happily Ever After* was the *source* of her dilemma?

"There are always little problems," Clarissa explained. "Take you and Mitch. I know you weren't happy on that trail ride. And so did your husband. But he was so eager to make it up to you, so ready to please you, that we fixed your problems without a hitch. But I've never, ever had a couple contemplate divorce. Not on their honeymoon!"

"Perhaps I could talk to Kelly Jean. Convince her to reconsider. Or at least give Kip another chance."

Clarissa reached out and took Lianne's hands in hers. "Could you? I know Kelly Jean just loves you. And Kip and Mitch have so much in common. If anyone can bring the two of them back together, you and Mitch can. I just knew you two were something special when you arrived."

"You did?"

Clarissa nodded. "I can tell these things. I have a sixth sense. I know you and Mitch will have a long and happy life together. Kip and Kelly Jean were a little iffy, and my doubts have proved right. But I'm sure we can get them back on the right track. Now, I better be off. I'll have to work on smoothing things out with the Saunders couple and the Conroys. We've got to nip this problem in the bud. After all, at the Pocono Pines, Every Honeymooner Is a Happy Honeymooner!" She guzzled down the rest of her beer, then stood up. "And I'll damn well make sure they are!" she exclaimed, slamming the mug down on the bar.

Lianne drew a long breath as she watched Clarissa Bliss hurry out. Her plans for Mitch would have to wait. Right now, she had to dig herself—and Kelly Jean—out of a huge marital hole. And the sooner she got Kip and Kelly on an even keel, the sooner she could turn her attention toward Mitch.

6

"I DON'T WANT TO TALK to him!"

Lianne stood on the porch of Kelly Jean's cabin, her forehead pressed against the rough wooden door. "Come on, at least make an attempt to work this out. Maybe you were a little hard on him."

The door swung open in front of her, and Lianne jumped back at the sight of Kelly Jean. Her eyes were red, and her short cropped hair stuck out in errant spikes all over her head. She wore a flannel nightgown and carried a box of tissues. "You're the one who told me to confront him!"

"I didn't tell you to slap him across the face with a fish. Or push him off the pier into the lake."

A tiny smile curved Kelly Jean's downturned lips. "No, I thought of that all on my own. You should have seen his face. I don't think he ever expected me to do that."

"You embarrassed him. There were a lot of people watching."

"There were, weren't there?" She rubbed at her red nose with a tissue, then tossed it over her shoulder. "But I'm not going to apologize. He's going to have to come to me and say he's sorry. I'm not going to be his sweet little Kelly Jean any longer. This Kelly Jean has a spine, and she's going to use it."

"Would you talk to him if he came to talk to you?" Lianne asked.

"I'd consider it. If he promised to be nice. And if he bothered to listen to what I have to say. And if he stopped treating me like some half-wit. And especially, if he threw away that stupid Harvard sweatshirt he's always wearing around the house. I hate that thing. Besides, he didn't go to Harvard, he went to the University of Wisconsin."

Lianne nodded. "All right. I'm going to find Kip and try to smooth things over. And when he comes back to the cabin, I want you to talk sensibly to him. No slapping and no shoving."

Kelly Jean waved weakly as Lianne hurried down the path. All she had to do was find Kip and convince him to go back to his wife and discuss matters in a calm and rational way. Certainly, given a little time, he and Kelly Jean could come to an understanding. After all, they had married each other for a reason, hadn't they? They must have loved each other.

But that's what she had thought when she'd married Mitch. They were supposed to love each other forever. And look where it had gotten them.

Over the next half hour, as the moon rose over the pines, Lianne searched the resort for Kip. But he was nowhere to be found. A nagging suspicion told her that he'd just dragged himself out of the lake and driven away, leaving his wife at the resort. But she checked with the bellhop and he assured her that he hadn't fetched the Albrights' car for either one of them.

Out of options and completely out of ideas, Lianne decided to see if Mitch could help her. He seemed to know the kind of guy Kip was. Maybe he'd know where the reluctant honeymooner was hiding himself.

With a new determination, she turned and headed toward their cabin. She'd never expected her advice to Kelly Jean to cause such problems. What was the big deal, anyway? She'd merely advised that the woman stand up for herself. There was certainly no way she could have predicted that this simple suggestion would reverberate so soundly through the Pocono Pines Honeymoon Resort. If it had, then there were a lot more marriages in trouble than she'd ever expected.

Or perhaps, it was just the pressure of the weddings and the honeymoons and the happily-ever-afters that had caused this spontaneous blowup. She remembered how she had felt in the weeks just before and after her wedding. So many changes, so quickly. A life-long commitment staring her in the face over the breakfast table. It had been difficult to adjust, to know if she was really, truly happy. Or if she was merely fooling herself into believing she was.

Wasn't anyone sure anymore? Wasn't there at least one newly married couple out there who was absolutely positive that they knew what they were doing? She wondered what that felt like, to be certain, without a shadow of a doubt, that the marriage was going to last. Even she had doubts on the day she married

Mitch, and no one had ever been in love the way she had—at least that's what she'd thought.

Lianne sighed and shook her head, then slowly climbed the front steps to the cabin. This really wasn't about her and Mitch. It was about Kelly Jean and Kip, and the other couples who had taken sides in their little battle. After all, she and Mitch were over, done. Their marriage was finished and merely part of history now.

"What the hell is going on here, Lianne?"

She jumped at the sound of his voice and turned to see him push his long, lean form out of one of the Adirondack chairs on the porch. He slowly approached, his gaze fixed on her, one eyebrow cocked up in curiosity.

Lianne pressed a hand to her heart and consciously willed it to slow down. He'd scared her, that's all. She wasn't reacting to the fact that he wore nothing but a pair of jeans, slung low on his narrow hips, or that the moonlight gleamed off his chest until she had to close her fingers into a fist to keep from reaching out and touching him.

"Were you waiting for me?" she asked.

He nodded, never once taking his eyes off of her.

"It's kind of chilly out here. Why didn't you wait inside?"

"Because Kip Albright is inside, smelling like dead fish and drowning his sorrows in our minibar. He's been here for the past hour."

Lianne drew a deep breath, then stepped toward the door. "Good, I have to talk to him."

He grabbed her arm to stop her from going inside.

"Wait just a minute. I'm not going to let you go in there. Haven't you caused enough trouble already?"

"Trouble?"

"You're the one who started this whole thing between him and Kelly Jean, aren't you." His words were not a question, but an accusation.

Lianne twisted out of his grip. "What do you mean?"

"I talked to Kip. He told me what Kelly Jean said. And everything he recounted sounded suspiciously familiar. That was *you* talking, not Kelly Jean. Annie, I warned you not to get involved in their marriage."

She rubbed her arm where the warm imprint of his hand still lingered. "Well, what was I supposed to do? She was sitting in the bar all teary-eyed. I just gave her a little advice."

"A little advice? About marriage? And just what qualifies you to be dishing out advice? We're divorced, or have you forgotten that fact?"

She scowled. "Don't say that so loud! For all we know, Clarissa Bliss has this place bugged."

"Well?" he said, more softly this time, drawing her closer. "We aren't married. And we haven't been for a long time."

"But that doesn't disqualify me from rendering an opinion. Even you have to agree that Kip can be a real jerk sometimes. Kelly Jean was just standing up for herself, the same way I should have stood up for myself after we got married," she said, anger seeping into her low voice. "Maybe then we—" She stopped short, not sure that she wanted to go on.

"Maybe then we'd still be together?" Mitch asked.

That's what she was about to say, but it wasn't what she wanted Mitch to hear. It wasn't that simple. Their problems couldn't be summed up with one "maybe then." "No. Maybe then it wouldn't have taken five years for me to figure out that our marriage wasn't working." She straightened, summoning up her resolve. "Our marriage is not the issue right now. Kip and Kelly Jean's is."

"He's not in the mood to talk to her," Mitch warned. "She walloped his ego pretty badly."

She gave him an incredulous look. "I'd say it needed a good dousing in a cold lake, wouldn't you?"

"I don't think you understand the dynamic here, Annie."

"Of course I do. Kip's a jerk and Kelly Jean deserves an apology."

Mitch shook his head. "No, you don't understand."

Lianne tipped her chin up stubbornly. "Then, why don't you explain it to me?"

He took her arm and dragged her with him, then gently pushed her down into one of the rough-hewn chairs on the far end of the porch. She waited for him to take a seat beside her, but he chose to stand, leaning back against the porch railing.

"Let me tell you how Kip feels. And for once, I'm speaking from experience, because this is exactly how I felt in the days before and after our wedding. See, Annie, guys like Kip and me are expected to get married. Our families drilled that into us from the time we were just kids. College, law school, marriage and then kids.

And of course, somewhere in that timeline, a nice house in the suburbs and a dog. Our parents were comfortably wealthy and, for the most part, happily married. We were expected to be the same."

He paused, then rubbed his arms as he gathered his thoughts. "But along with all that expectation comes an incredible amount of pressure. Will I be able to take care of my wife? What about when kids come along? What if I lose my job? How will I be able to pay the mortgage? So many people are depending on me, how will I be able to cope?"

She sat back in the chair and stared up at him. "There are two people in a marriage, you know. Your wife could have held up her end of the bargain."

"No," Mitch said. "That's not the way it's supposed to be done. At least not the way our fathers did it. It was all my responsibility, Annie. And in order to deal with that responsibility, I had to be the one to control it all. I had to be smarter and faster and more driven than everyone else out there. I had to ignore any problems that I sensed at home because I couldn't accept the fact that I might be failing in some way. I just worked harder and hoped all the problems would solve themselves, because I didn't have the time or the energy to deal with them. And even though I was beginning to detest the job that I was supposed to love, there was nothing I could do about it. I had responsibilities. I had you."

"We could have talked about this," Lianne said. "You could have come to me. I would have understood."

"No, I couldn't. My father handled his responsibilities on his own. And so did my grandfather."

"And my father and mother talked about their worries."

Mitch chuckled humorlessly. "But your family was...different."

Lianne bristled. "Why? Because they didn't have the money or the social position that yours did? Because they didn't have the huge house on Beacon Hill and a new car every three months?"

He looked at her, shocked by her words, a wounded look flashing in his eyes. "Of course not. Is that what you thought I meant?"

She shrugged, ashamed that she'd reacted so defensively. In all their time together, he'd never once made anything of her family's financial situation. His parents had, as well as his younger brother and sisters, but never Mitch.

"I meant that your family was open about their feelings. You talked about things. I didn't grow up in your household, Annie. In many ways, I wish I had. I didn't have that...luxury." He sighed and raked his hand through his hair. "I was twenty-five years old, I had a wife, and a life all laid out in front of me. And I was scared to death that somehow I'd screw up. And I did."

Lianne stood up and stepped toward him, then placed her hand on his arm. His skin was warm to the touch, and the warmth seeped from her fingers into the rest of her body. "It wasn't just you, Mitch. It was both of us. And beating yourself up about the past is not going to change what happened between us. It's over and that's it. Now, I think we'd both better concentrate on Kip and Kelly Jean. At least there's a marriage we can salvage."

Mitch nodded, then slipped his arm around her as they moved to the front door. She tipped her head and rested it on his shoulder, wanting to wait for a moment before they went inside, needing time to absorb all he'd told her. But Mitch pushed the door open and she had no choice but to step inside.

But she certainly didn't expect what was waiting for her when she did! She'd thought she'd find Kip, concerned and contrite, pacing the length of the cabin, prepared to beg Kelly Jean's forgiveness. Instead, Kip lay sprawled on the couch, drunk as a skunk and surrounded by little empty liquor bottles from the minibar. Along with wrappers from all the other items he'd eaten. The smell of fish wafted up around him.

"There she is!" he shouted, wavering a bit as he stood. "This is all your fault!" Tears swam in his eyes, and he angrily brushed them away. "She should never have listened to you."

Shocked by the fury in his expression, Lianne stepped back. Very calmly, Mitch placed her behind him and held out a hand to Kip. "Come on, man. Don't blame her. Your wife is the one who pushed you in the lake, not Lianne. In fact, Lianne was just over at your cabin trying to smooth things out with Kelly Jean. Don't you think it's about time you did the same?"

Lianne poked Mitch on the shoulder. "He's drunk. You can't send him back over there."

"I'm not going back," he said to Mitch. "You told me I could spend the night here, and that's just what I'm going to do. She doesn't deserve me, you know. I'm too good for her." With that, he flopped back down on the couch, groaned once and closed his eyes.

Lianne pushed Mitch aside and gave Kip a shake. But he only groaned again and rolled over on his side. She turned to Mitch, her jaw tight. "Kip cannot sleep on the sofa," she whispered. "*You're* supposed to sleep on the sofa!"

Mitch shook his head and leaned closer. "No," he countered in a soft, even voice. "*You're* supposed to sleep on the sofa. *That* was the deal."

She blinked, her gaze jumping between Mitch's resolute smile and Kip's half-conscious form. "You expect me to sleep with him?"

"Not on your life, sweetheart," he replied.

"Well, where am I supposed to sleep, then? How could you have given my bed to Kip?"

Mitch shrugged, then strolled across the room to the foot of the loft stairs. "After the fight we had earlier, I just figured you'd be sleeping with Kelly Jean at their cabin."

She hurried after him, her hands braced on her waist, her temper rising. "Well, what am I supposed to do for a place to sleep now?"

"I'd suggest you sleep with me, like a wife is supposed to do. Unless, of course, you want Kip spreading it around the resort that you and I aren't sharing the same bed."

With that, he turned and climbed the steps, leaving

Lianne with a definite quandary on her hands. She could stay awake all night long. Or she could spend the night with Kelly Jean, listening to her wail about Kip. She could probably even curl up in the hot tub if need be or sleep in one of the chairs on the porch.

But there was absolutely no way she was going to share a bed with her ex-husband. Not unless sharing that bed would lead directly to the seduction she had decided to pursue. And right now, she didn't think that Mitch was in any mood to be seduced, especially not by his ex-wife.

IT TOOK HER ONLY FIVE minutes to weigh her options and make the decision to climb the stairs. Mitch was turning down the covers and fluffing the pillows when she quietly walked over to the huge heart-shaped bed. He smiled inwardly, knowing how much of her considerable pride had to be swallowed just to make it up those stairs.

He gave her a sideways glance. "What side of the bed do you want? Would you like the left ventricle or the right? It used to be the right, or is my memory wrong?"

"You slept on the right," she said. "I slept on the left. But I always preferred the right. So I'll take the right."

"I guess it doesn't make a difference," he said. "I always end up in the middle, anyway." He pointed to the bed. "Go ahead. You can have the right."

She shifted nervously on her feet and twisted her fingers together in front of her, then hesitantly moved to her side. Mitch moved to the opposite side and lazily unbuttoned the top button of his jeans.

"What—what are you doing?"

He shoved the faded jeans over his hips, tempted to take the silk boxers right along with them. But considering what had happened that very afternoon, the sight of him naked might send her scurrying for the stairs and the safety of Kelly Jean's cabin. For now, it would be best to get her into bed first and then see what developed later. "I'm not going to sleep in my clothes." He looked up at her. "What about you?"

She shot him a stubborn glare, then began to unbutton her dress. "I don't plan to, either."

He didn't expect the sudden flood of desire that snaked through him at the sight of Lianne in her underwear. Fearing that his reaction would be all too obvious, he turned and rummaged through his duffle bag, then tossed her a clean flannel shirt. "Here," he said, surprising himself with the edge in his voice. "You can put this on."

She turned her back to him and he took a moment to study the delicious curve of her spine, the sweet shape of her backside, as she slipped out of her bra and into his shirt. When she faced him again, he couldn't help but imagine what the flannel covered, the swell of her breasts, and the smooth, silken skin of her belly and the wonderful pleasures that lay below.

She stared at him defiantly as she crawled into bed. Methodically, she pulled up the covers and arranged them around her, staying as close to her edge of the bed as possible. Biting back a smile, Mitch did the same, until they both were neatly installed in the bed.

They sat beside each other for a long time, neither one speaking, their eyes fixed on their toes. Mitch found the whole situation so ridiculous that he wanted to laugh, but he knew that would only fuel her temper. Lianne was not happy about their sleeping arrangements, that much he could tell.

He turned toward her, stretching out and bracing his head on his hand. The movement nearly sent her shooting out of bed. He quirked an eyebrow and watched her regain her composure. "Would you like the lights on or off?"

She cleared her throat. "Off, please."

He rolled over and flipped off the light, plunging the loft into a soft darkness. Seconds ticked by as he listened to her soft breathing. She didn't move, didn't speak, and he waited. Then, after several long minutes, she sighed and slipped down beneath the covers.

"Good night, Mitch," she murmured.

He paused, fighting the temptation to roll over and gather her into his arms. "Good night, Annie."

He closed his eyes and willed his body to relax. But the thought of her so close, close enough to feel the warmth from her body, was enough to set his nerves on edge and destroy all hope for a good night's sleep.

God, what he would give for just one touch, just one gentle brush of her lips. His mind flashed back to that afternoon, to the fire that had ignited between them in the dance studio and had flamed out of control behind the closed door of the cabin. Had that been just this afternoon? It seemed like ages ago.

He remembered the feel of her hands on his chest, the ease with which she could excite him, could draw him nearer to the edge. He placed his hand over his heart and felt it thud evenly beneath his fingers. Pinching his eyes more tightly shut, he tried to remember the details, tried to conjure up the image of her, half undressed, her hair wild around her flushed face, her hands skimming over his body.

A wicked flood of warmth twisted through his gut, and he felt himself growing hard beneath the sheets. His mind flashed an unbidden image of her long, delicate fingers wrapping themselves around him, surrounding and slowly caressing his hard shaft.

With a groan of frustration, Mitch sat up in bed and punched at the pillow. He cursed his errant thoughts along with the woman who lay beside him, then flopped back down on the bed and willed himself to sleep.

Mitch wasn't sure how much time had passed, but he was still fighting images of them, limbs twisted together, hands frantically exploring, when she softly called his name.

He didn't answer at first, not certain whether he'd really heard her or whether the sound had been a figment of his overactive imagination.

"Mitch? Are you sleeping?"

His breath caught in his chest, and he held it there for a long moment. Slowly, he let it go, pushing back the desire until he could handle the sound of his name on her lips. "I was," he lied.

"Oh, I'm sorry. Go back to sleep. I didn't mean to wake you."

He growled softly. "I'm awake, Annie. What do you want?"

"Remember earlier, those things you said about your family and the expectations and responsibilities?"

He waited for her to go on, his breath shallow in his chest, but she paused, expecting him to reply. "Umm," he murmured as he let the sweet sound of her voice invade his senses.

"I can understand how hard it must have been for you. And I'm sorry that you had to face that all alone."

He didn't answer this time, just listened and she rolled onto her side and faced him. He knew if he reached out, he could touch her.

"Why did you leave the firm?" she asked. "What happened?"

Mitch opened his eyes, his desire quickly forgotten, and looked at her, barely making out her form in the dark. "It's not something I like to talk about, Annie," he said, his words sounding cold and empty even to his own ears.

But she wouldn't be deterred. "I—I'd like you to tell me. It must have been something very serious to make you just quit a job that meant so much to you. I'd like to understand."

Her soft voice curled around him like a warm blanket on a chilly winter's day. She reached out and placed her palm on his pillow, so close she nearly touched his face. Slowly, he drew his hand up and covered her fingers with his.

"I got the case a few years after we got married," he began.

And so the story spilled out of him, every legal detail, and every emotion that he had felt. She didn't say a word, just listened as he told her of the little boy who had haunted his mind for more than five years, the boy who still had the power to turn his dreams into nightmares.

"When I told my father about the check, about cleaning out my trust fund, he went ballistic," Mitch said. "We had a huge argument and I resigned. I haven't set foot in that office since."

She pressed his hand between both of hers and wove their fingers together. "I heard about that story. It was on the news. I didn't know it was you." She paused. "You did the right thing, Mitch. I mean, giving them that money."

"I always thought of that money as our future, like insurance against anything that might go bad for us. But after the divorce, I really didn't need it."

"Even if we'd still been married, I would have wanted you to give it to that boy's family."

"But I wouldn't have. I would have felt that I couldn't."

She drew his hand closer and tucked it beneath her cheek. "We would have discussed it," she said in a sleepy voice. She yawned and he felt her warm breath on his arm. "We would have discussed it, and then we would have done it together. It was the proper thing to do."

He waited for her to say more, but her last words had drifted off, and a few minutes later he knew she had fallen asleep, his hand still pressed between hers. Carefully, without waking her, he moved closer, until their bodies were nearly touching beneath the covers.

He held his other hand over her arm for a moment, then touched her, softly stroking the skin below the rolled sleeve of his flannel shirt. He wanted her to wake up, to talk to him some more, to drive away the quiet of the night with her sweet voice. But she slept on, peaceful and soundless.

He leaned closer and pressed a kiss on her wrist. "But we wouldn't have talked about it," he whispered, her skin warm on his lips. "Not then. We didn't know how. But we do now." He took a shaky breath. "Only now it's too late."

LIANNE CAME AWAKE SLOWLY, first to the feel of his body curled against her back, and then to the gentle sound of his breathing. She smiled to herself and remained perfectly still so she might enjoy the moment a bit longer. It felt good to lie in his arms, safe, as if nothing could tear them apart.

Except for a loud pounding on the door. She pushed up on her elbow and looked at the clock. It was 10:00 a.m. Had they really slept that long? The pounding continued, and she gave Mitch a shake and slipped out of his embrace before he fully woke.

"What?" He squinted at her through bleary eyes, at

first uncomprehending and then slowly lucid. A sleepy smile curved his lips, and he reached out to pull her back into his arms. "It's not time to get up yet," he growled.

She evaded his hands and crawled out of bed. "Someone is at the door."

"Tell them to go away."

Another round of pounding began, this one loud enough to rouse Mitch into an upright position. He rubbed at his eyes. "What the hell is that?"

"I told you, someone is at the door."

With a long groan, Mitch tossed back the covers and crawled out of bed, then walked with her to the loft railing. They looked down at the door just in time to see Kip roll off the sofa, stub his toe on the coffee table and curse a blue streak. Still hopping on one foot, he flung the door open. Clarissa Bliss stood in the doorway, her clipboard clutched in her arms.

"Whadda you want?" Kip demanded, rubbing his sore toe and trying to keep his balance.

She gave him a distasteful sniff. "I'm here to invite you to join a few of your fellow newlyweds for a group discussion on constructive marital problem-solving."

Kip let his foot slip from his hand, nearly falling over backward in the process. "I wouldn't have anything to add to *that* discussion," he said, grabbing the edge of the door to slam it shut.

But Clarissa would not be deterred, and she shoved her foot against the bottom of the door. "Listen, buster, this is not an invitation, it's an order. I've spent good money to bring in the best marriage counselor on the eastern seaboard, and you're going to show up and listen to what she has to say. I'll be damned if I'll let you or any other nitwit newlywed ruin my reputation. You *will* come to the discussion group, you *will* listen, and you *will* make up with your wife. Do I make myself clear?"

Kip shifted back and forth a few times on his bare feet, then nodded.

"Good," she snapped. "I'll expect you in the White-tail Room right after lunch. Don't be late or I'll hunt you down like the dog you are."

Then, to Lianne's surprise, Clarissa turned her gaze up to the loft railing. "And you two will join us as well, won't you."

The last was said without any pretention of a request. Clarissa's smile had long disappeared, and her demeanor was that of a drill sergeant. Lianne and Mitch both nodded, neither one willing to incur the wrath of Clarissa Bliss, at least not this early in the morning.

She smiled her perfect smile. "Well, then it's all arranged." She reached out and patted Kip's arm. "We're going to have fun, you'll see. We're all going to be happy honeymooners before this day is over. Now, why don't you all spend some time making yourselves presentable and then come to lunch. I swear, Kip, you look like you've been run over by a truck." She looked up at Mitch and Lianne. "And I'm not sure what you two were doing last night, but I hope it wasn't sleeping!"

With that, she turned on her heel and left, leaving

the three of them to stare after her in astonishment. It was Kip who spoke first. "Geez, who lit a fire under her shorts?" He grabbed the door and slowly closed it, then turned to stare up at Lianne and Mitch.

"Don't look at me," Mitch said. "I intend to do exactly what she's ordered. And if you know what's good for you, you'll do the same."

Kip yawned, then nodded. "I need a shower. And some coffee."

Mitch stepped around Lianne and descended the stairs. She watched him cross the room and grab Kip's arm, then steer him toward the door. "You can take a shower in your own cabin. And you can get coffee at the restaurant. If I were you, I'd leave right now, before you completely wear out your welcome."

Mitch yanked open the door, pushed Kip out onto the porch, then slammed it behind him. Then he noticed his shoes and jacket on the floor, grabbed them and tossed them behind him. That task completed, he leaned back against the door and looked up at Lianne.

"I don't suppose there's any way we can go back to bed and wake up all over again, is there?" he said.

He looked so irresistible, wearing nothing but his silk boxer shorts and a sexy grin. She was tempted to take him up on the offer, but right now her mind was occupied with other things. "Clarissa hired a marriage counselor. I think that's a good thing for Kip and Kelly Jean. And the Conroys."

"And the Saunderses," Mitch added. "I heard they weren't on speaking terms, either. I have to say, Annie, when you take on a project, you don't do things half-way."

Lianne's smiled faded, and she shot him a withering glare. "None of this is my fault. If they hadn't argued here and now, they would have argued later." She paused. "I'm worried about this marriage counselor, Mitch. I mean, this person will be a professional. What if she can tell we're not really married?"

"I don't think it would be wise to skip the session," he said. "With Clarissa on the warpath, you never know what might happen. Besides, you should be there. After all, you're the reason we're all in this mess in the first place. I won't be surprised if Clarissa tacks the price of the marriage counselor onto our bill."

Lianne frowned uneasily. "You really don't think she'd do that, do you? I mean, how am I going to explain an expense like that to Mrs. Pettigrew? The magazine only pays so—"

"Annie, if I have to stand here looking at your naked legs a minute longer, I'm going to come up there and drag you back into bed. If I were you, I'd get my sweet butt into that bathroom and get myself ready for lunch, unless you'd like to deal with an ex-husband who has more on his mind than your expense report."

He made a move toward the stairs, and with a quick scream, Lianne scurried for the bathroom. Safe inside, she quickly locked the door behind her, then paused to consider what she was doing.

Why the heck was she running from him? Isn't that what she wanted, a full-scale seduction, no-holds-barred? What difference did it make whether she initiated it or he did? It would be just as wonderful either way.

Lianne reached out to unlock the door, then hesitated. Maybe now was not the best time. She had imagined something very romantic, candlelight, perhaps, and champagne, and a long, slow approach to the entire matter. Something that might soothe the nerves that she'd experienced last night when she'd crawled into the same bed with him. They were due at the dining room for lunch in less than an hour, and then at Clarissa's discussion group immediately afterward.

Lianne glanced at herself in the mirror and smiled conspiratorially at her reflection. There would be time later on this evening. Time to mull over her options and plan her strategy. For now, she would simply enjoy the anticipation.

She stripped off the flannel shirt and panties, then flipped on the shower and stepped inside the spacious, tile-lined stall, made for two. As she let the water sluice over her head, she allowed her imagination to wander.

What would she do if Mitch stepped inside the shower stall at that very moment? She tried to picture his body, tall and lithe, and without the benefit of his boxer shorts. A delicious shiver skittered down her spine. It could be so wonderful between them, so easy. An affair with absolutely no strings.

Her mind flashed back to the feel of him, in bed, beside her. She'd been tempted to give her plan a try last night. But Kip snoring on the sofa had a definite cooling effect on her desire. In all her fantasies, she imagined frantic passion and uncontrolled response—in other words, a lot of noise.

No, the stage had to be carefully set and they had to be completely alone. And if everything was perfect, it would happen just the way she imagined. A purely physical relationship with absolutely no strings.

After all, they both knew the mistakes they'd made in the past, and neither one of them was ready to jump into another relationship again, especially not with each other. This time it would be different, she assured herself. This time they would both know what they were getting into at the very start.

And if it didn't work out, then there would be no messy divorce, no ties to break, no legalities to deal with. They'd simply say goodbye and go their separate ways, neither one any worse for the experience.

Lianne smiled to herself and ran her fingers through her wet hair. Tonight they'd share the same bed, but this time, if she had her way, neither one of them would get any sleep.

7

"AND FINALLY, MITCH, why don't you tell the group what it is about Lianne that made you fall in love with her?"

Lianne felt herself sinking into her chair. She knew this question would reach the two of them sooner or later. After all, it had slowly made its way around the room to each and every other couple present. And with each response came tears and heartfelt declarations of true and everlasting love.

As Clarissa Bliss had promised, she'd brought in the best. Dr. Sylvia Skinner was a noted author and radio talk-show host, a person that Mrs. Pettigrew had quoted any number of occasions. In fact, Mrs. Pettigrew had been determined to convince Dr. Sylvia to write a question-and-answer column for *Happily Ever After*, addressing relationship problems that accompanied planning a wedding and learning to live together afterward.

Thank goodness all Eunice's attempts had been in vain, for if they hadn't, Lianne's cover would have certainly been blown this time. Not that it hadn't nearly disintegrated with all the questions Sylvia had been asking. Both she and Mitch had been on edge, hoping against hope that one of them wouldn't say anything to contradict the other. But after a time, it became obvious that Dr. Sylvia had been asked to focus her attention on more needy couples—like the Albrights. In Clarissa's mind, Mitch and Lianne were already on their way to a successful marriage.

"Mitch?"

Lianne's attention was drawn back to her "husband." All eyes were on him as he squirmed nervously in his chair.

"Is there a problem, Mitch?" Dr. Sylvia asked.

He forced a smile, and Lianne felt herself tense in anticipation. "Well, I'm just not used to talking about these things in public," he replied. "In my family, we pretty much kept our feelings to ourselves."

"That's all right, Mitch," Dr. Sylvia said, her voice calm and reassuring. "Do your best. Look at Lianne and tell her why you love her. Forget that the rest of us are in the room. It's just you two now."

Mitch turned to Lianne. Hesitant to begin, he took her hand in his and studied her fingers for a long moment. She winced inwardly, knowing that he had to be scrambling for a suitable answer, hoping that it would sound convincing. Catching his gaze, she sent him what she hoped was an encouraging look and then prayed that he'd keep his wits about him.

"I've never really told Lianne that I love her," Mitch began. "I mean, I have, but I've always waited until she said it to me and then I'd just mumble the same back to her. In my family, we never said those words, never out loud and never spontaneously. It was just assumed, so I assumed that Lianne would know how I felt."

"Did you know how he felt, Lianne?" Dr. Skinner asked.

Lianne opened her mouth, then snapped it shut, not sure of what she should say. She blinked hard. Were they talking about her real marriage, or was this just make-believe? How was she supposed to answer? "Yes," she finally said. "I guess I knew that he loved me. Although I noticed that he never said it without prompting."

"How did that make you feel?"

"Unsure?" Her answer was more a question, for she wasn't truly certain how it had made her feel. She'd never verbalized those feelings before. Sometimes angry, sometimes sad, and usually a little empty. What she did know was that when it came down to it, when she had been ready to walk out the door of their town house, even then, he hadn't been able to say the words. "I guess I just tried not to let it bother me. But it did. It hurt."

"Why do you love Lianne, Mitch? Go ahead and tell her."

He drew a deep breath while she held hers, then began very slowly. "I love Lianne because no matter what happens, I always know she'll be on my side. She has this incredible loyalty, an absolute trust that makes me believe the best about myself, that makes me want to do better every day of my life. Not in the financial sense, or the professional sense, but in the way I treat other human beings.

"There was a time, a few years back, when I didn't trust her to stand by me, when I'd begun to believe I wasn't worthy of her loyalty or her love. So I shut her out of my life, let her walk away, but I don't think I ever stopped loving her. In fact, I know I never did. I love her more today than I've ever loved her before."

Lianne felt her heart twist at his simple words, then chided herself for feeling anything at all. He didn't really mean what he was saying. They were simply words spoken as an actor might speak lines in a romantic scene. But her mind spun back to their conversation the night before and the story about the little boy.

A slow realization dawned. Was that what had driven them apart? He'd told her how he'd hated himself for his part in the whole thing. Had he hated himself so much that he'd allowed her to walk out on him, that he had let her go without telling her how much he really loved her?

"See how easy that was? When we talk calmly and rationally about our feelings we can work through any problem. But we also have to remember what it is that holds us together. Love." Dr. Sylvia smiled and stood up. "There will always be hard times, that's part of marriage. When your problems seem insurmountable, always come back to the love you have for each other. That will help you through anything you may encounter."

With that, Clarissa Bliss popped out of her chair and started a rousing round of applause. Many of the couples stopped to speak with Dr. Sylvia before leaving, but Mitch and Lianne snuck out the door as quickly as they could. Lianne was anxious to put the charade behind them once and for all, and to regain the relative safety of their cabin.

As they walked silently along the lake, Mitch slipped his hand around her waist in a gesture that had become almost second nature. Create the perfect picture, she thought to herself. She risked a glance up at him, but he was staring straight ahead, his mind a million miles away.

She cleared her throat, then looked out at the lake. "The water looks so blue today, doesn't it?"

He looked down at her. "What?"

"Nothing," she said. "I was just commenting on how pretty the lake was."

He gave the landscape a halfhearted gaze, then shrugged. "I guess it is."

"So, what did you think of Dr. Sylvia Skinner?"

He fixed his eyes on the trees. "I thought she had some interesting things to say. She managed to solve Kip and Kelly Jean's problems without any bloodshed. They were holding hands during most of the session." He paused. "Are you hungry? Clarissa said they would be serving dinner a little later for us. We can go now if you'd like."

Lianne shook her head. "I ate a few of those cookies she was pushing. I can't believe we were in there for such a long time. Almost six hours. But I guess Miss Bliss wasn't about to leave anything to chance. If you're hungry, maybe we could go back to the cabin and order room service?" She mentally reviewed what she'd order. Maybe some fresh strawberries and whipped cream. And a bottle of champagne.

Champagne was always a necessary component in a proper seduction, and she was still determined to go ahead with her plan, even though she had found the afternoon's events a bit distracting.

"Actually, I'm not too hungry myself. I was thinking I might turn in early."

Lianne stumbled slightly, and a look of concern crossed his face as he grabbed for her elbow. But she quickly recovered. "It's only seven o'clock," she said, desperate to convince him that the night was still young.

They'd reached the front steps of the cabin, and Mitch turned to her. "I didn't get much sleep last night. And sitting in that discussion group, trying to come up with plausible answers all afternoon, kind of wore me out."

Lianne didn't know what to say. This was not what she had planned! In every fantasy she'd had, there had never been a point where Mitch chose a good night's sleep over the allure of her attempted seduction. She just wasn't doing this right.

"Why don't you stay up for a bit? I thought we might be able to talk," Lianne offered.

He shook his head wearily. "I'm really beat, Annie. We can talk in the morning. If you want some company, why don't you go down to the bar. Maybe Kip and Kelly Jean will be there."

"I'm sure Kip and Kelly Jean are locked in their cabin, making up for lost time." *Which is what we should be doing,* she thought to herself. All this talk about going to bed early, about getting some sleep. It was just—

She blinked as a bolt of realization struck from the blue. Maybe it was his way of proffering an invitation! They'd slept in the same bed last night. Did that mean he expected the same tonight? Perhaps all this talk about sleep was merely a ruse to get her in the vicinity of the bedroom. Good grief, she could be obtuse at times.

Anxious to test her theory, Lianne grabbed the door and pushed it open. "Now that I think about it, I am a little tired. I'd like to go to bed, too."

He followed her inside and closed the door behind him. Then he slowly walked past her toward the loft stairs. As an afterthought, he reached out and brushed a chaste kiss on the top of her head. "I guess since Kip's gone home, the sofa is all yours again. Sleep tight, Annie."

She watched in utter bafflement as he trudged up the stairs. A few moments later, when she heard him flop down on the bed, her heart sank. How could this be happening? Hadn't he been the one who was pushing her toward something more intimate? The teasing, the kisses, yesterday in the dance studio and in the cabin afterward? He'd wanted her then, so what had suddenly changed his mind?

Her thoughts wandered back through the events of the last few days, and she tried to put her finger on the exact moment when it had all gone wrong. Sure, they'd fought over Kip and Kelly Jean, but no more than they'd fought over anything else on this trip. And last night, in bed. They seemed to grow closer as they spoke and she'd been certain the only thing keeping them apart had been the unwanted presence of a guest on their sofa.

She cursed softly. But tonight...tonight was supposed to be the night when it all came together, when she'd toss aside her reticence and doubts, when he'd finally be overwhelmed by his desire, when they'd tear up the sheets until the early morning hours.

And nothing was going the way she'd planned! Lianne glared up at the loft. Well, she was not going to let this stop her. If he didn't know what was on her mind, then she'd damn well tell him. Now! Before she lost her nerve.

Drawing a deep breath, she stalked across the room and stamped up the stairs. As she rounded the railing at the top step, she froze. He was lying on the bed, his back against the headboard, his long legs crossed indolently. He wore just his jeans, the button undone at the waist. His chest and his feet were bare.

"Hello, Annie," he drawled. "The sofa a little lumpy? I figured it wouldn't take you long to demand the bed back. You had that look in your eye."

She stiffened. "That's not why I'm here."

His eyebrow cocked up and he smiled. "Then why are you here?"

Lianne took a slow, deep breath, her gaze never wavering from his. Her heart slammed inside her chest, but she summoned her determination and willed it to slow down. She could do this. It was really quite simple when she thought about it.

She reached for the buttons of her blouse and worked them open, one by one. With each button, his smug smile faded by degrees, until, when her blouse slipped from her shoulders and puddled on the floor, his expression was rigid, his eyes dark.

He pushed himself up in bed. "What the hell are you doing, Annie?" His voice was raw with disbelief. "I wouldn't start with me, if you know what's good for you."

"I'm not starting anything," she said in an even voice, a tone she could barely keep from cracking. "I'm finishing what we began in the dance studio."

"But I thought—"

"I changed my mind," she said, reaching for the button on the back of her flowing cotton skirt.

He cursed beneath his breath. "Sweetheart, don't tease me."

Lianne unzipped her skirt and let it fall around her ankles, leaving her in just her bra, panties and shoes. Impatiently, she kicked off the shoes and stepped out of the skirt, then slowly approached the heart-shaped bed. A surge of wicked power skittered through her body as she watched his expression change from suspicion to shock.

She wanted to shock him even more, so she arched her neck back and stretched her arms over her head, rumpling her hair in the process. Never in her life had she attempted anything so overtly enticing, but desperate times called for desperate measures.

Gone was the Lianne he once knew, the woman who had been happy with the obligatory three-times-a-week sex. She wanted things to be different between them, passionate and frantic like they'd been just yesterday afternoon in the cabin. They were in a different time and a different place, a place where the past could be forgotten and all their wildest fantasies could be played out on a heart-shaped bed in a cabin in the woods.

She watched him, smiling her most seductive smile. At first she thought he was going to resist, but then a low growl rumbled in his throat. He reached out and snagged her waist, then tumbled her into bed with him. With a tiny cry, she fell across his lap, and before she knew it, his mouth was on hers. What was left of her inhibitions slowly dissolved and she returned his kiss in full measure, demanding the same as he did, a perfect melding of their lips and tongues.

All that passion from the previous afternoon came back in a sudden flood. This time she wanted to linger over every instant, to ignore the restless need that burned deep inside of her. But need was greater than her resolve, and it begged to be sated before it burst into flames and devoured her. "Don't stop," she murmured against his mouth, skimming her hands over his shoulders.

"What do you want, sweetheart?"

"I want it all. Everything we've never had."

He tore his mouth from her, then branded her throat with his lips. "Ah, Annie, I've never felt this way before. Never needed you so much."

As he rolled her over and pinned her to the bed, coherent thought shattered into a million sensations.

Though she tried, she could focus on nothing except his body pressed against the length of hers and the delicious taste of his mouth.

His hands cuffed hers above her head, and he held them there as his mouth drifted away from hers. She twisted beneath him, but he wouldn't let her go. Slowly, he traced a path from her neck to her breast, then brushed his lips over her hard nipple. Separated by the filmy fabric of her bra, it was little more than a fleeting sensation. She cried out.

Mitch released her hands, and Lianne immediately furrowed her fingers into his thick, dark hair. She drew him back to the spot, and when he teased at her nipple with his tongue, she felt her limbs go boneless.

Why? Why had they waited so long to enjoy these exquisite pleasures? They'd wasted so much time, been apart for so long. It was as if they were made to be together, their passion meshing so perfectly. Yet that passion had remained hidden until now, buried under layers of propriety and confined expectations, suspended for five years while they found their way back to each other.

"Take it off," she pleaded, tugging softly on the hair at the back of his head. "I don't want anything between us."

With frantic fingers, Mitch tore at the satin bra until she felt the heat from his lips on her bare skin. Her panties followed, shredded with reckless abandon, and his hand slipped lower on her belly. She reached for his jeans and struggled with the zipper. With an impatient curse, he pushed up and stood beside the bed, then stripped them off.

Her breath died in her chest at the sight of his naked body, of his hard arousal. He stood there for a long moment, watching her, their gazes never wavering. "Are you real?" he murmured, his voice catching with barely held self-control. "Is it you or someone I've never touched before?" She reached out and drew him back onto the bed. He lay down beside her and threw his leg over her hips.

"I'm real," she murmured. She placed his palm on her heart. "See?"

"This is not the same," he said.

"It's not supposed to be. I don't ever want it to be the same."

His hand stroked her hip and he pulled her closer. Aching for his touch, she pushed his palm up to her breast, and when he cupped her, heat surged through her. "I want your hands on me," she murmured desperately. "And I want to feel you inside me."

She felt him tense for a moment, then he groaned softly and slid his hand back to her waist. She slid his hand back to her breast and she opened her eyes. "What is it?"

He cursed vividly. "I didn't bring anything to— Hell, they've got to sell the damn things somewhere at this resort."

"Don't worry," she murmured. "I've got that covered." He gave her a dubious look, and she moved his fingers back to where they belonged. "I stayed on the

Pill after the divorce. I was optimistic I'd have a reason for them."

His jaw tightened, and she saw a brief flicker of jealousy in his eyes. "And did you?" he asked, his tone even.

Lianne smiled and traced his bottom lip with her finger. "Not really. At least not until now."

He relaxed and nuzzled her neck. "Good. I don't relish the thought of beating off a gang of surly boyfriends for the exclusive pleasure of making love to you." He paused. "It will be exclusive, Annie. As long as we're together it's just you and me. No one else."

With a lazy sense of exasperation, she sighed. "I'm tired of negotiating with you, counselor. Just shut up and make love to me. I think we've waited long enough."

She had made love to Mitchell Cooper hundreds of times before, but she'd never made love to this Mitch Cooper. He was wild and hungry and out of control. They rolled across the heart-shaped bed, moaning and gasping, frantic to get closer, to feel every inch of each other, skin against skin, soul meeting soul.

She laughed low in her throat, and he responded, his words urgent. She teased, making him groan in pleasure. And she whispered in his ear all the things she wanted him to do to her, all the fantasies she wanted fulfilled.

And when he couldn't take any more, he grabbed her wrist and slowly showed her what he wanted. "Touch me," Mitch growled. "Touch me, Annie."

With a delicious sigh, she wrapped her hand around

him and slowly began to stroke his heat. He sucked in his breath and she stopped, sensing that he was so close that she might bring him there with nothing more than her fingers. He cursed softly, then pulled her on top of him, his muscles tense, his eyes dark.

She smiled as she slowly impaled herself, luxuriating in every hot and hard inch of him. And then, as if they were of one mind, they began to move, the desire building between them until she could feel it humming in her ears.

One moment, she was greedy, wanting him to draw her closer to her peak. And in the next, she was giving, bringing him along with her. And in the end, they came together, arching and crying out, and then tumbling down, until the climax subsided and they were sated.

MITCH ROLLED OVER in the heart-shaped bed, kicking at the tangled covers. Spreading his arms out to either side, he opened one eye and then the other, then closed them both and groaned.

She wasn't in bed with him. He must have dreamed the entire thing. Lord, what a dream. It had far surpassed any fantasies he'd ever had, as a teenager or a fully grown man. Sunlight streamed through the window and spilled onto the bed. He pulled a pillow over his face. The scent of her perfume touched his nose and he smiled sleepily.

It hadn't been a dream. The state of his body told him that. Every muscle had been tensed and relaxed so many times that he felt utterly exhausted and wonderfully satisfied.

Lianne had come to him and she'd stayed with him, in the huge bed, for that incredible night and all of the next day and another night, the hours melding together in the heat of their passion until they couldn't tell day from night. They'd lived on lovemaking, wild, incredible sex, punctuated only by long, quiet conversations, room service and mind-numbing sleep.

He'd never expected it, not in a million years. He'd opened his heart to her in front of Dr. Sylvia and everyone else, and had watched her face for some reaction. But she had remained coldly composed, as if his confession hadn't affected her in the least. It was then that he'd decided there had been no chance for them, that every ounce of feeling she'd once possessed for him was now completely gone.

So as they had walked back to the cabin, he'd resigned himself to failure. No matter how strongly he felt about her, she could never love him again. Then she'd come up those loft stairs and caught him completely off guard. He had thought they were about to argue over the bed again. But events took a very unexpected and pleasant turn and he knew his words had gotten through to her, that they'd meant something.

A song drifted up the loft stairway and Mitch smiled, listening to her off-key rendition of "You Made Me Love You." Lianne had never been much of a singer. But then, he'd never thought of her as much of a seductress, either, until now. After what had passed between them, he wasn't sure that he would ever judge her so quickly again.

He heard her turn on the whirlpool jets, and soon her singing increased in volume and was accompanied by softly bubbling water. His mind slowly formed an image of her, naked as she delicately stepped into the tub and slipped down into the warm water.

With a low laugh, Mitch crawled out of bed and padded down the stairs, the morning air cool on his nude body. He found her stretched out in the tub, her head tipped back, with bubbles up to her neck.

"Is there room in there for me?"

She opened one eye. A smile teased at the corners of her mouth. "I suppose I could make room. Are you as bone-tired as I am?"

He stepped into the water, then slid onto the seat next to her and wrapped his arm around her shoulders. Sighing, she turned and leaned back against his chest. "God, this feels good," he murmured. "Can we stay here all day?"

Lianne shook her head. "We'll turn into two old prunes," she said.

"I like the sound of that."

She giggled and slapped his wandering hands away. "We can't stay. I have plans."

He looked down at her flushed face and watched a drop of moisture trace a track from her temple to her jawline. "Do they include me?"

"Umm. I signed us up for that rock climb you wanted to do. Since this is our last day here, I thought we'd better get it in before we leave. I might never have a chance like this again. And I'm in the mood to try something new and adventurous. You've turned me into a reckless woman, Mitch Cooper."

Mitch touched his lips to hers. "What if I told you I don't give a damn about climbing rocks right now? I'd much rather climb back into bed with you."

"I would tell you that you're allowed ten more minutes in this tub before we get dressed and get down to the lodge. I really want to do this."

"Since when?" Mitch asked.

"Well, I had been gathering some information on adventure honeymoons back at the office. You know, rugged, outdoor destinations. Everyone always thinks of pampered luxury on a honeymoon, but I think we have some readers who'd like something a little more exciting, maybe even a little dangerous. I had thought it would be hard for me to get the feel for these destinations, but with your help, I'm sure I could do a good job."

"With my help?"

She looked up at him, concern coloring her eyes. "You haven't forgotten our deal, have you? Four weeks for the Mustang. You've got three weeks left before I sign over the title. Do you think you'll have trouble getting off work?"

Mitch warmed at the thought of another three weeks of travel with Lianne. Another three weeks of relaxing days and incredible nights. Hell, he'd quit his teaching job and sling hamburgers if that was the only way he could go along. "I'm sure it will be no problem. When do we leave?"

She rubbed her palm across his damp chest. "We haven't finished this assignment yet. Now I'm going up to take a quick shower and get dressed."

"Can I come with you? I'll promise to wash your back."

Lianne laughed. "Have you forgotten what happened the last time we took a shower? We were in there for over an hour, and room service had to come back twice."

Mitch closed his eyes and tipped his head back to rest on the edge of the tub. "I remember quite vividly."

He heard her climb out of the tub and turned to watch her walk, naked and loose-limbed, toward the stairs. "Ten more minutes and I'm coming to drag you out," she warned as she dripped water across the floor.

"I'll look forward to it," he murmured to himself.

He relaxed in the steaming water, letting his mind wander languidly into the future. It had been an incredible week, but tomorrow they'd go back to Boston and they'd—

He stopped and frowned. What *would* happen between them? In all their conversations over the past twenty-four hours, they'd never talked about it. Would they see each other during the week and on weekends, like steady companions usually did? He didn't like the sound of that. Or would they move in together, sharing a small apartment while they both worked, but free to leave at any time? The sound of that had even less appeal.

He wanted Annie back in his life—permanently. To risk losing her again was unthinkable. He sighed, resigned to the fact that there was only one logical solution. He was in love with his ex-wife, and to that end, he intended to marry her all over again.

His problems solved, Mitch submerged himself in the bubbling water for a long moment, then surfaced again. Now all he had to figure out was how and when he'd ask her to marry him. And of course, the methods he'd need to employ to get Annie to say yes.

HER FINGERS DUG INTO the rough rock as Lianne tried to maintain her toehold.

She should have never looked down. Mitch had been repeating that very thing to her since she took her first reluctant step up the sheer rock face. Look up and keep climbing. Feel the rock with your feet and your fingers. There is nothing to be afraid of.

"You're doing fine, sweetheart. There's a handhold just above your right hand."

She risked a glance over at him, then felt a wave of vertigo. She pressed herself flat against the rock and slid her fingers up to grasp it. There really was nothing to be afraid of. She and Mitch were climbing the face side by side, helping each other over the difficult spots. Besides, the Pocono Pines took no chances with its guests. They were firmly strapped into harnesses that were attached to lines, and they could easily be lowered back down the forty-foot rock face by the two well-muscled instructors.

"Why don't you two take a break," one of the instructors called down from the top. "Just push away from the rock and dangle for a while. It will give your muscles a chance to recover."

Mitch looked up and waved, then did as he was told. But Lianne clung to the rock face, afraid to move. The first few feet had been fun. When she'd hit the ten-foot mark, she'd decided that the rest of the climb would be a breeze, no more difficult than climbing a ladder. At twenty feet, she had made the mistake of glancing down, and that's when the fear took hold.

Mitch had been so patient with her, helping her along, giving her advice and encouragement. But with every step she took up, all she could think about was going back down. Thank God, there were just the two of them. Rock-climbing at the Pocono Pines was not one of the group activities.

"Annie, you can let go," he said. "They've got us secured from the top. You won't fall, trust me."

"I don't want to let go," she muttered. "I'm going to stay right here where I'm safe. I'm planning to spend the night here, and tomorrow morning they can send a helicopter for me. The pilot can drop me off at the manicurist."

Mitch laughed. "The harnesses will hold you. And even if it doesn't, you could jump from here and probably wouldn't break anything. We're only twenty feet up."

Lianne felt her temper rise. He might be willing to drop twenty feet onto hard-packed ground, but she certainly wasn't. In fact, she'd had just about enough rock-climbing for one day. "Mitch, I want to go back down. Tell them to let me down," she said.

He swung over to her and gently rubbed her back. "Are you sure? We don't have that much farther to go. I'm sure you can do it. You've done really well so far."

"*Can* isn't the issue here, it's *want*. I don't *want* to do it, it's as simple as that."

Mitch gave her an indulgent grin and shrugged. "All right, I'll tell them you want to go down."

"Wait!" Lianne bit her bottom lip. She was acting like the old Lianne, afraid and unsure of herself, and she hated that side of her. Heck, she'd done things a lot harder than climbing up a cliff on the end of a rope. But no matter how much she wanted to make herself take one more step up, she couldn't make her hand move. "So much for danger and adventure," she muttered. "I suppose you're disappointed in me, aren't you?"

Smiling, Mitch reached out and brushed the hair off her damp forehead. Their eyes met, and she felt that familiar, comfortable warmth pass between them, banishing her fear and her vertigo for a brief instant. He chuckled softly. "Disappointed? Where would you get a silly idea like that? Sweetheart, do you have any idea how much I love you? I don't give a damn if you climb this rock or not."

Her heart stopped in her chest, and she suddenly found herself searching for a breath. Her knuckles turned even whiter as she gripped the rock and pressed her cheek into the rough surface. "What did you say?"

"I said, I don't give a—"

"Before that," Lianne interrupted.

"I said I love you," Mitch replied. "In fact, now that

we're on the subject, there's something else I want to say."

She forced a laugh that sounded strained and false. "Mitch, this isn't the time to talk about these things. I'd better go down now."

"Annie, this is the perfect time. I've got you to myself, and you can't go anywhere until I give the word. Why not here?" He cleared his throat, then slid a bit closer, grabbing on to an outcropping to hold himself in place. They both lay flat against the rock now, their faces just inches apart. "Annie Cooper, I love you. There's no getting around that fact, and to tell the truth, I don't think I ever stopped loving you. I was stupid not to tell you how I felt, and because of my stupidity, we wasted five years of our lives together. I want you to marry me, Annie, for the second and last time. And we're going to dangle here until you say yes."

"Mitch, I—"

"Say yes," he repeated.

Lianne drew a shaky breath and fought back a wave of tears. No, she would not cry, especially not here and now. She swallowed hard, looked up, and then looked down. There was no escape. She'd have to tell him now and get it over with. "No," she said softly, "I won't marry you, Mitch."

His face was a mask of disbelief. "I don't understand. What do you mean you won't marry me?"

She brushed her damp eyes against her upper arms, still clinging to the rock. "Just what I said. Now, I think I'd like to go down, if you don't mind."

"The hell you will!" His angry voice echoed against

the cliff and she winced, wondering if the instructors could hear everything they said. "What about last night and the night before that? Annie, we made love, and don't tell me it didn't mean anything to you."

"We had sex," she clarified. "At least, that's what I had. And it did mean something to me. It meant a lot. But never once did it mean that I wanted to marry you again."

"And why not?" he demanded. "Don't you love me?"

Lianne paused, then answered as honestly as she could. "Of course I love you. I've always loved you and I always will. But I don't want to marry you again."

"Why not?" he insisted.

"Do I have to go over all the reasons? Let's just say that it didn't work the first time, and it probably wouldn't work the second or the third or any other time you wanted to marry me." She looked up at the instructor, who peered over the edge in curiosity. "I want to go down now," she shouted.

"No, she doesn't," Mitch countered. He turned back to her, his expression angry and confused. "And what are we expected to do? Just pretend that this never happened? Or do we just pick up where we left off at the next honeymoon destination? A great vacation, hot sex, and then we call it a week."

He made it sound so tacky, but that was the option she considered most practical. "Would that be so bad? You have your life and I have mine. We've spent five years apart, Mitch. I don't think either one of us is going to be lonely. Why can't we just take this for what it is? We had a deal, or don't you remember?"

"Screw the damn deal," he cursed. "And just what the hell were you taking this for?"

"An affair. We're having an affair. It's not uncommon for ex-spouses to continue to be attracted to each other. But that doesn't mean we should jump back into marriage because we've got the hots for each other. It didn't work then, what makes you think it will work now?"

"Because you and I are different people. We've changed."

"Maybe I have. But you're still trying to railroad me into marriage, the way you did ten years ago." She looked up again. "I'm ready to go down now!" This time her demand was more insistent. "And don't listen to my husband," she said. "He doesn't have a clue as to what I want."

"Don't do this, Annie. Don't walk away from this."

She felt the rope give a bit, and drawing on her courage, she pushed away from the rock. Inch by inch, she and Mitch grew farther apart as the instructor lowered her off the rock face. "I can't marry you," she called softly. "And I don't want you to ask me again. If you decide you can accept me on my terms, then we have something to discuss. If not, I don't have anything more to say to you."

And with that, she left him, clinging to the side of a cliff, not certain whether he'd climb up or down, toward her or away from her. Perhaps she'd wanted him to love her all along, and perhaps she'd even wanted to prove to herself that she could get him back. But now, faced with the prospect of opening herself up to the same old dangers, the same unbearable pain, she wasn't sure what she wanted.

All she was sure of was that she needed to get as far away from Mitch Cooper as possible—starting right now.

8

SHE HAD TOSSED her clothes into her suitcases without folding them and hopped on the first courtesy van to the Lehigh Valley airport. In less than an hour, she had been on her way back to Boston, back to the safety of her little apartment and the security of her life there.

Clarissa Bliss had been concerned, but Lianne told her that she had to leave because of a family emergency and that Mitch would stay until tomorrow and drive back. She quickly paid the bill and left the Pocono Pines Honeymoon Resort before Mitch had a chance to corner her again.

The ride to the airport and the flight back home had passed in a blur. But now that she was in the familiar surroundings of her apartment, her mind had begun to clear, and the numbness that had kept her emotions at bay had started to wear off.

Lianne placed her palm on her chest and rubbed, trying to rid herself of the ache that seemed to surround her heart. It shouldn't hurt so much, she repeated to herself. Leaving him this time wasn't nearly as bad as when she walked out on him five years ago. Then, why did it feel that way? Why did it feel as if her heart had been torn in two?

With a soft curse, she grabbed her suitcases and

dumped her clothes out on her bed, then studied them distractedly. The dress that she wore that day in the dance studio brought back an instant flash of remembrance. And to her dismay, she realized that she had packed the T-shirt that Mitch had lent her that first night they shared a bed. She picked it up and crushed it to her nose, wondering if it might still hold a trace of his cologne or the scent of his shampoo. Then, when she realized what she was doing, she tossed it back on the pile.

How could this have happened? How could she have been so stupid? She thought she understood Mitch, at least enough to assume that he harbored nothing more than platonic, if somewhat intimate, intentions toward her. He was the one who couldn't bring himself to tell her he loved her all those years ago. He was the one who let her walk out on their marriage without a single word of protest.

She should have known something had changed almost from the start. His gentle teasing, the affectionate gestures in his apartment that day. But she wrote them off as a simple flirtation from a man who had become much more relaxed in her presence now that they weren't married. Old friends teased each other and they were only friends. Or at least that's what she thought.

When it went further, when the flirtation turned to desire, she told herself that Mitch's attraction to her was purely physical, the result of two adults sharing close quarters. She'd been convinced that was all there was to it. Even when he dropped the first clue, she'd completely ignored it.

Or maybe she'd heard it but refused to believe it. Her mind replayed the words he'd said to her that night in Dr. Sylvia's discussion group. He'd told her then what he felt, and she'd assumed he'd been playing his part as her adoring husband. *I love her more today than I've ever loved her before.* Lianne felt a sob catch in her throat and she fought it off. Why now? Why had it taken him this long to realize his feelings? She had put her love for him behind her and hardened her heart against ever allowing herself to feel so deeply again. How could he expect her to instantly forget the past, forget the hurt and the sense of failure she had felt when their marriage had crumbled, and go running back into his arms?

She'd thought she had it all figured out, thought they'd be able to enjoy a little fling, then go on with their lives. Right! Who the heck did she think she was fooling? Deep in her heart, she knew she wanted more and a casual affair was only an excuse, an excuse to keep the hurt and pain, and the blooming hope, at bay.

This was all her fault. She had gotten herself into this mess and now she was paying the price. She'd practiced deception, lying about her marital status at work, taking the promotion when she knew Mrs. Pettigrew would never have hired her in the first place if she'd known about the divorce.

It wasn't important that Mrs. Pettigrew was wrong to require her staff members to be married. And all she really wanted to do was provide a little extra money for her parents. But a lie was a lie, and sooner or later, lies always came back to bite a person in the backside.

But worst of all were the lies she had told herself. About her ability to resist him, about the feelings she no longer had for him, and about the paralyzing fear that he would hurt her again.

She snatched up her black sandals from the bed and tossed them in the direction of the closet. What had ever possessed her to pick up that phone and call his office? He'd been out of her life, finally and for good, and she'd drawn him right back in again, all in the name of keeping a job she should have never been given in the first place.

Lianne glanced at the clock. It was nearly 9:00 p.m., and suddenly she felt numb with exhaustion. She had called her parents from the airport, and they had promised to drop Irving off after they'd done their regular Friday night grocery shopping.

She smiled wistfully. It was all the entertainment they could afford these days, strolling the aisles together, comparing prices and discussing products. Hopefully, they'd have melting ice cream in the car and wouldn't stay too long. Right now, she just wanted to crawl into bed and put the events of the past week far behind her.

She sat down and picked through the clothes that still remained as she tried in vain to harden her emotions. What was she so upset about? She had convinced herself once that she didn't care for him and she could certainly do it again.

Closing her eyes, she flopped back on the pillows.

She could lie to Mitch, but she couldn't lie to herself. She couldn't count the number of times she'd fantasized about a second chance with him, an opportunity to see if they could make things work. And when he'd proposed, hanging from the side of that cliff, there had been a tiny, wonderful instant when she had rejoiced, before her instinct for self-preservation had kicked into high gear.

Mitch had been her first love. And her only love. Since their marriage had dissolved, every man she looked at had been held up against him and found sorely lacking in comparison. And yet, when it suited her, she could tear him apart, fault by fault, until she'd convinced herself that he'd never been a man worth loving in the first place.

Back and forth she had gone, until, after a few years had passed, the ache of losing him had diminished. She had told herself so many times that she didn't love him, she had begun to believe in her delusion. But then he'd said the words, words that brought it all back again.

I love her more today than I've ever loved her before....

Marry me, Annie. Marry me...marry me...marry me again.

She pressed her hands to her ears. Words like that were hard to ignore, for they echoed in her mind, over and over until she wanted to scream. No, she couldn't ignore them, because deep in a secret part of her heart, in a place she had refused to acknowledge for more than five years, she still carried a tiny seed of her love for him.

She held the seed in her hand now, and she knew that simply by confessing to its existence, she could no longer deny her feelings for him. Yes, she still loved him. And all her talk about a simple affair between the two of them was just talk. In her heart, she wanted it to lead to more. And if she planted the seed and let it flourish, that love would grow. It would be different from before, stronger, more resilient, and much more brilliant in color.

She closed her hand and then opened it again, and the seed she imagined was gone. It would be different, but could she guarantee that it wouldn't end up exactly the same? Could she risk her heart once more in an attempt to love the man she knew Mitch was, the man at the very center of his soul?

Lianne buried her fingers in her hair and pressed the heels of her hands into her temples. No! She couldn't risk her heart again. It had shattered into a thousand pieces once before, and she'd managed to paste it back together. She would never survive a second time.

"I'll forget him. I'll put him out of my mind. There'll be no casual affair. And I won't get hurt again."

The doorbell rang, and Lianne looked over at the bedside clock, then pushed herself up off the bed. Irving would be thrilled to see her, and she'd be just as happy to see him. He'd drool all over her and then all over the apartment, and finally, he'd jump up onto her bed and drool on that. But in the middle of the night, he'd be there beside her, one constant in her shifting life. At least some things never changed, she mused.

Lianne hurried to the front door and flung it open,

prepared to fend off Irving's enthusiastic welcome and his slobbering tongue. But the dog and Lianne's parents weren't on the other side. Instead, she found Mitch Cooper.

"What are you doing here?" She gripped the edge of the door with a white-knuckled hand, ready to slam it shut.

"We need to talk, Lianne, and it might as well be now." He stepped inside. "I've decided to take you up on your offer."

He looked awful. His eyes were rimmed in red, and little lines of tension radiated from the corners of his mouth. He wore the same clothes he'd worn for their climb, and considering the time, she figured he must have left the resort not more than a few minutes after she did.

"My offer?"

"We'll do it your way. No strings, no expectations. And no mention of marriage."

"No," Lianne said, shaking her head. "That offer is off the table."

He clenched his fists at his sides. "What the hell does that mean? You told me that's what you wanted."

"Well, it's not what I want anymore," she replied. "I've changed my mind." A hopeful look flooded his face and her heart twisted. "I don't think we should see each other anymore, Mitch. I think that we should just call off the deal we made."

"You can't do that," he said. "A deal's a deal."

"Yes, I can since it's my deal, my rules. You can keep the Mustang. I'll mail you the title. I'll keep sole custody of Irving, and we'll go on like nothing ever happened."

He reached out and grabbed her arm. "But something did happen, Annie, and you know it. Denying it won't make it go away."

"Nothing happened," she said, yanking out of his grip. "We slept together. We spent a few...nice days—" she swallowed hard "—and nights with each other, but now the honeymoon is over. It's time to get back to the real world."

"Damn it, Annie, don't lie to yourself. I was there. I felt it as strongly as you did. It's not over between us, not by a long shot. There's still something there. I know it. We still love each other."

Lianne drew a deep breath, gathering her resolve. "Please, Mitch, don't make this difficult for me. For both of us." She turned and glanced at the clock above the sofa. "My parents are due here any minute. I don't want them to see you. It will only upset them. Please, just go. And don't come back."

He cursed softly, then raked his fingers through his hair. "I'll go for now," he conceded, "but I'm not going to give up. I know you love me, Lianne, and I refuse to lose another day living without you."

"Go," she pleaded.

He reached out and brushed his knuckles along her cheek. She closed her eyes, fighting off a flood of tears.

"Go."

"This won't be the end of it."

When she opened her eyes again, he was gone. And

so was a huge piece of her heart, a piece she suddenly wanted back, along with the man who had stolen it.

"GOOD MORNING, LIANNE. Welcome back! Mrs. Pettigrew is waiting for you in your office."

The receptionist in the lobby of *Happily Ever After* gave Lianne a bright smile and an oddly expectant look. Lianne frowned as she strode down the hall, her heart hammering in her chest. Her first day back to work and Eunice was waiting? Had something happened? Had Mrs. Pettigrew somehow found out about her deception?

She steadied her nerves as she neared her office, rationalizing her fears. After everything that she'd been through, she was prepared for a short and well-deserved firing. The truth be told, she'd spent all day yesterday composing and recomposing a letter of resignation. She had taken the position under false pretenses, and if Mrs. Pettigrew required her employees to be happily wed, then Lianne did not qualify in the least.

She could find another job. After all, she now had nearly five years of magazine experience. She had only one week as a full-fledged editor, but she'd just work her way up to that once again. Everything would be fine, she murmured to herself. Lianne Cooper had weathered much worse and survived.

The door to her office was closed, and she hesitantly reached out to push it open, anxious to get the whole thing over with as quickly and painlessly as possible. But the sight that greeted her was not at all what she expected. There was no tight-lipped Mrs. Pettigrew waiting to lower the ax. Instead, Eunice stood in the middle of a flower-filled office, a beatific smile on her face.

"Lianne! Darling! Look at this!" she gushed. "Isn't it just the most romantic thing you've ever seen?"

For an instant, Lianne could barely make her boss out as her rose-patterned dress became lost among the roses crowding the desk. She drew a deep breath. Her office smelled like a floral shop, an exotic mélange of so many different scents, one was indistinguishable from the other. Roses, daffodils, mums, lilies. They were all represented in the mixture, and more.

"You—you didn't have to do this, Mrs. Pettigrew. I mean, I'm grateful for the promotion, truly grateful, but—"

"You think I did this?" Eunice laughed gaily. "Don't be silly! I didn't buy you these flowers. That sweet man you married did! I must say, Lianne, you certainly caught yourself a fine one. I've never seen a husband so devoted to his wife's happiness as your Mitch."

"My Mitch?" she murmured, taking in the opulent and very expensive bouquets. "My Mitch did this? But that's so—" She was about to say, unlike him. "Nice," she finished. "How nice of him."

Eunice clasped her hands over her heart. "I must say, I couldn't have chosen a better honeymoon editor. With all the romance in your life, it's as if you and Mitch are still on your own honeymoon."

Lianne gathered her courage and forced a smile.

"Actually, Mrs. Pettigrew, that's a subject that I'd like to—"

Her boss waved her hand. "Not now, dear. Enjoy the moment, stop and smell the roses. We'll talk about your trip later. I know all I need to know, and that's that you two had a wonderful time." She inhaled deeply then sighed. "I've never met a more romantic man," she said as she bustled out. "Except, of course, Mr. Pettigrew."

Lianne stared at the empty doorway, then slowly turned to take in the contents of her office. "I don't believe this," she muttered.

"Neither did I."

She spun around. Shelly stood in the doorway, a sly smile on her face.

"I assume the honeymoon went well?" Her eyebrow arched speculatively. But she could restrain her curiosity for only so long before she giggled and rushed in, closing the door behind her. "All right, tell all. How long did it take before you two ended up in bed together?"

"Shelly!" Lianne tried to come up with a shocked look that might dissuade further questions, but she failed miserably. She suspected a guilty expression was all she could manage.

"Come on, Lianne. If you can't tell your best friend, who can you tell?"

"I shouldn't tell anyone, I'm so ashamed."

Shelly wriggled impatiently.

"All right," Lianne snapped. "Four days. Are you satisfied?"

"Gee, I would have thought you'd hold out longer. I would have bet on five."

"We were still in bed on the fifth day."

Shelly rubbed her palms together, then scurried to take a seat in one of Lianne's guest chairs. "Should I get coffee?" She hesitated, then waved her hand and settled into the chair. "No, I'm too anxious to hear. Was it as good as you remembered it?"

Lianne groaned. "Shelly, I really don't think—"

"Sit!" her friend ordered, shoving aside the flowers on Lianne's desk. When they could see each other, she gave Lianne a nod, as if it was all right to proceed.

"The truth be told, I never remembered it as being this good. And it..." Lianne paused as a delicious shiver skittered down her spine. "It was not good. It was incredible. Mitch and I were like two different people. That's the only way I can describe it. There was nothing left from the past—it was all new and... exciting."

"So, now that you and your ex have done the dirty deed, what are you going to do about it?"

Lianne couldn't help but smile. Leave it to Shelly to cut right to the chase. "It's over. The last thing I want to do is pursue a relationship with him. It didn't work the first time, why would it work the second?"

"Because you're different people," Shelly replied.

"What?"

"You said it yourself, Lianne. A lot can happen to a person in five years. Look what's happened to you. You're independent, you have a great career, you're living on your own. And what about Mitch? He's left his family's law firm. He's left all that money, he's..." She frowned. "Well, maybe we all can't make positive changes in our life, but—"

"But he has," Lianne insisted. "He's changed so much that there were moments when I barely recognized him. He used to be so rigid, so closed off with his feelings. So boring. And now he just blurts out whatever is on his mind. And he laughs and curses and fumes, sometimes all within a few minutes of each other. He's reckless and spontaneous and everything I used to want him to be. We were hanging from the side of a cliff, and he just turned to me and asked me to marry him. Just like that!"

Shelly gasped. "He what? Do you want to say that again? I'm not sure I heard you right."

"He asked me to marry him," Lianne repeated, surprised at the tremor of excitement that ran through her while saying the words. "He asked me to marry him," she said once more, the impact of his words slowly becoming real to her.

"And what did you say?"

Lianne bit her lip and shrugged. "I said no. I acted like the old, wimpy Lianne and ran away from it all. It took me five years to figure out that the old Mitch Cooper was not the man I wanted to be married to. And it will probably take another five for me to get it through my thick head that maybe this Mitch Cooper is the man I wanted all along. I don't know. I'm just so confused about it all."

"But you're going to marry him again," Shelly said. "You're going to say yes?"

"No," Lianne said.

Shelly's expression fell. "But you can work out all your confusion after the wedding."

"I'm going to take my time and decide if everything I feel for him is real. Shelly, I can't just jump back into marriage with him. That would be irresponsible and just plain foolish." She glanced around the office, admiring the flowers and wondering where he had found the money to pay for them. A tiny smile touched her lips when she realized she didn't care. He'd obviously chosen them all himself, owing to the bizarre mixtures in some of the vases. "But maybe I might give him another chance to prove to me that we could make it work."

Shelly nodded. "Ah, make him suffer a little. I like that idea."

"I just need time," Lianne said. "This has all happened so fast, so unexpectedly. I have to sort it all out. We can date for a while and see how it goes."

Her friend glanced around at the bouquets of flowers spilling from every available surface. "If it goes anything like this, you two will be married inside a month."

Lianne shook her head. "The last time I saw him, we had a huge argument. It's going to take a lot more than flowers to convince me."

Shelly opened her mouth to reply, but Lianne's intercom buzzer interrupted her thoughts and she snapped her mouth shut. Lianne pushed on the speaker button and answered the summons from the receptionist.

"Your husband is here."

The words echoed through her office, and she felt her heart skip. Mitch was here? She drew a long breath. Of course he was here. He'd sent the flowers and now he wanted to check if they'd had any effect on her feelings. With a trembling hand, she depressed the intercom button again. "Send him in, Jane. He knows where my office is."

Shelly popped out of her chair. "I guess that's my cue to leave. I'll be right next door with my ear pressed against the wall. Make sure you and Mitch speak clearly so I can understand every single word that's said. And remember, this is an office in which lovemaking on one's desk is not only allowed, but encouraged."

Lianne laughed nervously. "Get out of here, right now. And don't come back." She stood and rounded her desk. Shelly playfully hurried out, waving her hands in mock fear.

Lianne reached the door at the same moment Mitch did, and they both froze, standing only inches from each other. She could hear her heart thudding and wondered if he could, too, then decided that she'd better move before the heat from his body and the scent of his cologne completely unnerved her. A step back was all it took to break the spell.

"I see you got the flowers," he said.

She snuck a peek at his face, then joined him in appreciating his gift. "They're wonderful. I was surprised. But you didn't have to do this, Mitch. They're so—"

"Expensive?" A wicked grin curved his lips. "I still have my credit card from Cooper, Cooper and Cooper. I figure when it comes to you, my father owes me big time."

They both smiled, and an uncomfortable silence grew between them. Finally, she decided to speak. After all, she'd had a small change of heart, and perhaps it would be best to explain that to him, to—

"Actually, I came to see Mrs. Pettigrew," Mitch said. "But she's busy for the next few minutes, so I decided to stop by and see you."

Lianne stiffened. "Mrs. Pettigrew? What do you want with Mrs. Pettigrew?"

He crossed his arms over his chest and idly scanned the office, avoiding her gaze. "We have several important issues we need to discuss."

Her temper tweaked, she narrowed her eyes in suspicion, then reached around him and gave her office door a shove. Just what was he up to now?

"She's my boss, Mitch," she said in a low voice, "and I demand that you tell me what you plan to say to her."

He leaned back against the door and regarded her with a lazy smile. "You demand?"

"Are you going to tell her about us?" Her anger building, Lianne turned and began to pace her office. "This is just like you! I wouldn't do things your way and now you're going to resort to blackmailing me, for the second time, I might add."

"It's actually the third," Mitch said, "but who's counting."

"You're going to walk in there and tell her everything, that we're not married, that I lied to her, that I don't deserve this job." She stopped her pacing and faced him defiantly. "Well, go ahead. Tell her everything, Mitch. Spill the whole story, because holding it over my head is not going to make me marry you." She reached around him and whipped open the door. "Her office is down the hall, last door on the right. Enjoy the moment!"

He cocked an eyebrow in surprise, then opened his mouth to speak but decided against it. Lianne fumed, tapping her foot impatiently. If Mitch Cooper knew what was good for him, he'd get out of her sight as quickly as he could.

Thankfully, he did as she demanded and she slammed the door behind him. Her resolve had returned in full force, and she was not about to grant him even the tiniest bit of credit. He was a full-fledged scoundrel, not at all the sweet, honorable man she had believed him to be. In fact, the truth be told, he'd swung from one extreme to the other, spending less than a week as the Mitch Cooper she truly wanted.

"You're better off," she mumbled.

And to think she'd come so close to falling for it all. Well, Mitch Cooper was about to find out that even a roomful of flowers couldn't endear him to his ex-wife. She was glad she had divorced him, and she had every intention of maintaining her current marital status regardless of what enticements he tossed her way!

MITCH TOOK A SEAT on a delicately embroidered chair placed near Eunice Pettigrew's desk. He scanned her office, trying to contain the uneasy feeling that he'd mistakenly stepped into her boudoir. He was accustomed to thinking of an office as dark mahogany paneling and floor-to-ceiling bookshelves filled with orderly rows of books. But Mrs. Pettigrew's office more closely resembled the bed-and-bathroom boutique he'd wandered into at the mall while looking for a soap dish. Clutter, clashing prints and a cloying smell of old roses.

Potpourri, he thought. Lianne used to spread it all over their town house during the holidays. He never told her how the scent gave him a headache. Hell, he had never told her a lot of things.

Now that he had, he had hoped things would change between them. But obviously, telling her how he felt about her was having no effect. It was time to change tactics. No more talking, now he'd show her.

He heard the office door open, and Mitch twisted in his chair to watch Eunice Pettigrew bustle in. The instant she saw him, she smiled and held out her hand. "Mitch! So good to see you. How did you enjoy your week in the Poconos?" She waggled her finger at him. "No, no, you don't have to answer. I saw the flowers you sent Lianne. What a lovely and romantic gesture! I was just telling Lianne that I don't think the honeymoon is over for the two of you yet. Even after…how many years have you been married?"

"Ten," Mitch said, glad for the opportunity to speak. "Actually, Mrs. Pettigrew, I—"

"Eunice," she insisted. "Even though I am Lianne's boss, I feel as if you and I are kindred spirits. There are not many true romantics left in this world, are there?"

Mitch shook his head.

She sat down at her desk and folded her plump hands in front of her. "Now, dear, what is it I can do for you?"

He leaned forward and braced his forearms on her desk. "I need some help, and I thought that you'd be the perfect person to come to."

"Go on," Eunice said, her curiosity piqued.

"Well, next Friday is our tenth anniversary. And I wanted to plan something special for Lianne, a little dinner party. Since I don't know many of her friends, I was hoping that you might be able to put me in contact with a few of them here at work. I don't want to leave anyone off the guest list by mistake."

Eunice could barely contain her excitement. She clapped her hands together, then reached for a note-pad. "An anniversary party! Oh, how wonderful!"

"Just something small," Mitch insisted. "Just a few friends."

"I'll do better than that!" she cried. "I won't just help you with the invitation list, I'll plan the party. And it won't be just a little dinner party. We'll have a big celebration. In fact, we can cover it for the magazine! I've always believed that an anniversary celebration is just as meaningful as the wedding itself. And ten years of marriage is certainly something to be proud of!"

Mitch held out his hand to slow her enthusiasm. This was not what he wanted. He simply wanted a gentle reminder, so to speak, that the vows they had taken ten years ago still meant something to him. He knew if he invited her to dinner, she'd never agree to come. But if it was a party with a few of her friends, she couldn't possibly refuse. "I'm not sure I want anything that splashy."

"I insist," Eunice said. "Leave all the details to me. Since we're going to cover it for the magazine, I can expense the whole thing." She placed her finger on her cheek and her expression turned pensive. "Now, where will I be able to get invitations done overnight?"

With that, Mitch knew that he was completely out of his element. Perhaps it was best to leave everything to Eunice. With her considerable experience in the areas of love and romance, she was sure to do a better job than he would. Either way, his goal would be accomplished. He and Lianne would celebrate ten years of marriage—and divorce—together.

Mitch pushed himself out of his chair. "I really appreciate this, Mrs.—I mean, Eunice. And I think Lianne will as well. As for the cost, just—"

"Just leave it to me!" she finished, already reaching for the phone. "If you have any concerns or ideas, just call. But I'll take care of everything else."

Mitch had nearly reached the door when he turned around. There was something that had been bothering him since the day he'd first visited the *Happily Ever After* offices. And now was as good a time as any to bring it up. "I do have one question. Or perhaps it's more of a concern."

Eunice looked up from dialing the phone. "What is that, dear?"

Mitch crossed the room to stand over her desk. "Lianne tells me that all the staff members at *Happily Ever After* are married."

"Oh, yes!" Eunice said. "We pride ourselves on that

fact. But we do have a few people on staff who are engaged to be married."

He gave her the same look he'd used so effectively in the courtroom, the steely-eyed one that made witnesses cringe. "You realize that requiring a person to be married as a condition of employment is against the law. I know this because I'm a lawyer."

Eunice's bright expression turned to astonishment. "Against the law?"

Mitch nodded. "I'm afraid so."

Mrs. Pettigrew placed the phone back in the cradle with a clatter. Her hands fluttered over her desk, nervous, like a trapped bird. "I've been breaking the law?" She twisted her hands together to still the shaking. "But I've never broken the law in my entire life. Not even a speeding ticket. You can't be serious. This is a wedding-and-honeymoon magazine. It only makes sense to hire people who understand what it's all about."

"That's not what the government says," he replied.

Her face was stricken, as if the revelation were too much to bear. A sliver of regret shot through him, and he wondered whether he should have told her at all. Or maybe he should have approached the whole matter with a little more finesse. Hell, sooner or later someone was bound to bring a lawsuit. Better him than a greedy attorney with the means to wipe out everything she had built for herself.

"What am I going to do?" she asked. "Should I write a memo? Maybe I should call a staff meeting and apologize. I have to do something. I don't want my staff believing I'm nothing more than a criminal."

Mitch reached out and touched her trembling fingers. "My legal advice would be to keep your mistake to yourself. If you've never actually verbalized this requirement, you may be all right. There's nothing you can do to change the past, but before this week is out, it might be to your benefit to hire a few single or divorced staffers. Whether you need them or not. And from now on, marital status has nothing at all to do with hiring. Do you understand?"

Eunice nodded. "I do. I'll do that. I'll go right out and hire some single and divorced people." She stood up and circled her desk, then enfolded Mitch in her arms, pressing him into her ample bosom. "I can't tell you how grateful I am for your advice, Mitch. So very grateful."

Mitch slowly extricated himself from her embrace and forced a smile. Great advice, he thought to himself. Advice that nullified the trump card he held in his hand. Without a reason to pretend to be married, Lianne was free to flaunt her divorced status at will. He wondered how long it would take before a few more staffers came clean, as well.

By his measure, he had no more than a week, maybe two at the most, before the office grapevine conveyed the news. Just one week to convince Lianne that nothing she could say or do would deter him. He was a man in love, and he wasn't going to settle for anything less than a lifetime commitment.

"SHE'S DOING WHAT?"

Lianne leaned over the table and clutched at Shelly's hand. Her friend smiled wanly, twirling her straw around in her glass of lemonade. They'd appropriated their regular booth at the small sandwich shop just a few blocks from the office, a place where they lunched at least once a week. But this time, Shelly's invitation had been more than just casual. Lianne could now understand why.

"I thought I should tell you," Shelly explained. "I'm the one who's supposed to bring you to the party, but for the life of me, I couldn't figure out a way to get you over there without telling you the truth. Eunice has planned a tenth anniversary bash for you and Mitch. The magazine is going to cover the whole thing as part of a feature on anniversaries."

"And it's tomorrow night?"

Shelly nodded. "I'm sorry I didn't tell you sooner, but it was just such a romantic idea. I guess Mitch was the one who thought of it first, and when he mentioned it to Eunice, she just took it out of his hands. I feel sorry for the guy. He had such a sweet idea, and it's turned into this big extravaganza à la Eunice."

"Why would he want to plan a party?"

The waitress appeared with their lunches, a cheeseburger for Shelly and a chicken salad sandwich for Lianne, then discreetly left them to their conversation. Shelly grabbed her burger and took a big bite. "Maybe because you've refused to talk to him since he showed up at the office that day?" she said between mouthfuls. "Maybe he figures a party will flush you out in the open, so to speak. After all, how can you refuse to attend your own anniversary party?"

Lianne's eyes narrowed, and she twisted her napkin in her lap. "This is so like him. Using my friends and co-workers to get what he wants. I can't believe he's taken advantage of Eunice like this."

Shelly waved her hand, her mouth full, then swallowed hard. "I think it's more the other way around. She just loves this kind of stuff. Besides, she's got this great idea for a feature in the magazine, and you and Mitch happen to fit into her plans. Believe me, there will be plenty of pictures of the food and the party favors and centerpieces. Nobody will even notice you and Mitch. And the rest of the staff will act as window dressing, background for the photos. We've all been instructed to bring our spouses, probably so that the party looks more realistic. Jackets and ties only."

Lianne cursed softly. "He's backed me up against a wall again, Shelly! Either I play out this ridiculous farce of a marriage or I break down and tell Eunice the truth. Geez, she'll blow a gasket if she has to cancel her party. How am I going to tell her?" She tapped her spoon on the table as her mind spun with alternatives.

"Of course, I can't tell her. Not yet. And he knows that. The man always has all his bases covered."

Shelly reached across the table and patted Lianne's hand. "At this point, with all the money Eunice has thrown into this, I doubt if she'd cancel. She'd probably just find someone else to play the happily married couple for the evening."

"Then I'm going to tell her and I'm going to do it today," Lianne said. "She's planning this whole thing for us and there's no point."

"You may be wrong there," Shelly said.

"Mitch and I aren't married, so we shouldn't be celebrating an anniversary. That's a fact. The lies have gone on long enough."

"I mean, you may be wrong about the need to tell Eunice the truth."

Lianne frowned, searching Shelly's face for a clue as to what she was talking about. "Why is that?"

Shelly bent closer, her burger still clutched between her fingers. Lianne knew she was about to relay a bit of office gossip in her usual manner of communication—a conspiratorial whisper. "I heard, on good authority, that Eunice just hired a new assistant in the art department." She paused, as if to heighten the effect of her revelation. "And she's divorced." Shelly took a bite for emphasis, then slowly chewed as she waited for Lianne's reaction.

When her words finally registered, Lianne gasped, then shook her head. "No! That can't be. How did you learn that?"

"Debra in the art department heard this new girl

mention it when she was taking the grand tour with Eunice. Debra figured that would be the last she'd ever see of that candidate, but the girl showed up for work this morning. She told Debra Eunice hired her. It seems Eunice was quite sympathetic when she heard about this girl's marital woes."

"This can't be right," Lianne cried. "You must have misunderstood. Maybe Eunice misunderstood. You know how adamant she's been about this issue. All of us know. How is it she's suddenly done a complete one-eighty?"

"I don't know," Shelly said. "Maybe someone told her what she was doing was illegal? At least now I won't have to regale her every few weeks with sappy stories about my loving husband. I mean, I've got an imagination, but trying to turn Eddie into Prince Charming has been tough. He's been a frog for so long, he's growing webs between his toes. Although, I think that could also be due to the fact that he never takes his socks off, even in bed. I'd swear he showers with his socks on."

A slow smile spread across Lianne's face. "Do you know what this means?"

"That I don't have to wash as many dirty socks?"

"No! I'm talking about Eunice's change of heart. It means that I *can* tell her the truth. Now, today. I can tell her that Mitch and I are divorced and I'll be able to keep my job. I can tell everyone and stop living this lie."

Shelly shook her head. "But you can't tell her until after the party. You should at least give the guy a break. After all, Mitch wanted to do this just so he'd have a chance to talk to you. And I think you owe him that."

"I don't owe him anything!" Lianne cried.

"I think you might. I heard another interesting tidbit from Mrs. Pettigrew's secretary. It seems that Eunice's sudden change of heart came minutes after she and your ex-husband met last week. Now, considering that your husband is a lawyer and knows the law pretty well, I'm wondering if he told Mrs. Pettigrew that her hiring policies were discriminatory."

The thought struck her like a sharp slap to the face. Could Shelly be right? Mrs. Pettigrew's hiring practices had bothered Mitch from the start. In fact, he'd wanted to say something the first day he'd shown up at the office. Could he have mentioned something to her during their meeting?

She ground her teeth. It was exactly like Mitch, too! Barging in and spouting out his legalities until everyone agreed to play fair and square. Riding in on his big white lawyer's horse to save the day for everyone.

But slowly her anger toward him dissolved, replaced by a nagging feeling of gratitude and admiration. Once again, Mitch had helped her out of a jam, saved his damsel in distress. He had done it when he had agreed to pose as her husband, and now he'd done it again, both times doing what he could to save her career.

And losing whatever leverage he held against her. Lianne frowned. Surely he must have realized that once the truth came out, he could no longer control the battle between them, could no longer play her worries against her desires, the lies against the truth.

She stared down at her sandwich and picked at the wilted lettuce with her fork. Maybe he didn't want to fight anymore. Maybe he just wanted her to be happy. Without their secret, there was nothing holding them together—except their feelings for each other. Feelings she'd been trying awfully hard to ignore for the past week. And feelings he'd been determined to act upon.

"Mitch would do something like that," Lianne finally said. "He's always had a very strong sense of right and wrong."

The truth was, she missed him. Missed seeing him every day, talking to him about small, inconsequential things. She missed looking into his handsome face and running her fingers through his dark hair. But most of all, she missed feeling loved and cherished and desired. And that's how Mitch made her feel, as if he were simply desperate to be with her.

She had no doubt in her mind that if Eunice hadn't agreed to change her policies, the papers initiating a lawsuit would have been on her desk within twenty-four hours. He would have moved heaven and earth and the entire legal system to make it right for her.

"He saved your job," Shelly said simply. "How can you not love a guy like that?"

A grudging smile twisted Lianne's lips. "Who said I didn't love him?" she asked.

Shelly put on a shocked expression and dropped her cheeseburger on her plate. "Well, thank God, the light's finally gone on! I was wondering when you were going to get around to facing the truth. All this talk about needing time to think and making mistakes all over again. I was ready to slap you silly."

"Well, I'm still concerned about that. And I'm not completely convinced that we can make this work. But I guess I'm more open to giving it a try, now that my professional worries have been solved."

"You know, if you married him again, you'd never even have to tell Mrs. Pettigrew the truth."

Lianne laughed sharply. "Now, there's an idea. Marry my ex-husband to save me the embarrassment of fessing up to my deceptions. That's as good a reason as any to get married."

"You love him, don't you? I say, marry the guy. Don't waste another minute apart."

Lianne leaned back against the smooth red vinyl of the booth. Shelly made it sound so simple. Maybe it was. Maybe Lianne was the one throwing all the obstacles in the way. What if the mistakes of the past didn't make a difference? How would she feel if she could strip away all their history together and act on just the simple love that they had for each other? Would she agree to marry him then?

She sighed as an image of the two of them, in the heart-shaped bed, drifted through her mind. A tiny thrill of excitement vibrated through her, and she smiled to herself. What would it be like to have that passion every day of her life? To wake up every morning knowing that the man beside her had fought to have her, and to keep her?

Perhaps it was time to put her fears aside and find out.

MITCH STOOD ON THE BANK of the Charles River basin and watched as a single rower glided over the glassy water in his scull. A thin mist hovered over the surface of the river, the early morning air so still that he could hear each breath the rower expelled, could count the creaks of his oar locks.

He reached down and tugged at the front of his sweatshirt, then wiped the perspiration from his face. It had been a perfect morning for a run. Cool and quiet, an antidote to his restless night. He had paced his apartment until nearly 3:00 a.m., trying to come up with some way to make Lianne understand how he felt, how desperately he loved her.

He sighed inwardly. Why should she believe him? Why now, after all that had passed between them? Simply because he had told her he loved her, those three simple words that he'd neglected during the entire time they were married? No, there would have to be another way to show her.

Tonight was their anniversary party, a grand event that Mrs. Pettigrew had thrown her heart and soul into planning. He'd received a copy of the engraved invitation and a memo from Eunice's secretary detailing the party favors, the menu and a request for a list of Mitch and Lianne's favorite songs.

Somehow, his simple scheme to get Lianne to see him had turned into a major event, and he wasn't even sure the guest of honor would show up. As far as he

knew, she hadn't been told of the party, for Mrs. Pettigrew believed that it would be much more romantic to
surprise her. She'd be surprised, all right.

He had heard nothing from her since that day in her
office. He'd tried to call her, but she had always managed to evade his phone calls both at home and at
work. The two times that he'd stopped by her apartment, she'd refused to answer the door. And when
she'd seen him waiting outside her office building,
she'd turned around and gone back inside.

Mrs. Pettigrew had babbled on with her advice on
how to keep the party a surprise, telling him that he
was not allowed to visit the office again for fear that his
expression might give it away. So he had to settle for
the chance that he might catch sight of her in a
crowded subway station or on the street. He was like a
man lost in the desert, parched for just a brief glimpse
of paradise.

For all he knew, tonight might be his last chance to
plead his case again. He'd taken a big gamble, and he
wasn't certain how it would play out. If the staff had already found out about Mrs. Pettigrew's enlightened
hiring policies before the party, Lianne would probably opt for the truth, making their anniversary party a
moot point.

But if she hadn't heard, she'd do one of two things—
go along with the party, thinking it was the only way to
save her job, or tell Mrs. Pettigrew the truth right after
everyone yelled "Surprise!"

A one in three chance was all he had, Mitch mused.
Tonight and that was it, because if she didn't know

about Eunice's change of heart by the end of the evening, he was going to have to tell her. He couldn't keep it from her any longer.

She had to make her choice while in possession of all the facts, including the information that there was no longer a reason to perpetuate this facade of happily married bliss. If she wanted him—no, if she loved him—she was going to love him free and clear, without any lies standing in their way.

Mitch drew in a long breath and let it out slowly, the moisture clouding in the crisp morning air. Tonight was the night. If he couldn't convince Lianne to marry him by midnight, then all that experience pleading lost causes in front of stone-faced judges and impassive juries would go to waste.

He picked up his pace and began to jog again, heading down a small commercial boulevard not far from his flat. He nodded to an elderly man who was unlocking the front door of a jewelry store, and continued running. But when he got to the end of the block, he stopped and looked back at the store, a tiny mom-and-pop operation with a weathered wooden sign.

By the time he'd jogged back to the shop, the old man had already stepped inside and locked the door behind him. Mitch rapped on the window, and he saw the venetian blinds part. "We're closed," the man said.

"It's my tenth wedding anniversary today," Mitch replied. "I need to buy a gift. Can you open early, just this once?"

The eyes peering through the blinds gave him a suspicious look and then a careful once-over before Mitch heard the lock click. The door slowly swung open, and the old man motioned him inside. "Can't be too careful these days," he said. Bent from age, he hobbled through the showroom, pointing to the empty glass cases and scratching his head. "We put all our stock in the safe at night. What did you have in mind for a gift? I'll go get it out."

"I'm not sure," Mitch said, following along after him. "Aren't there special gifts you give with each anniversary? What's traditional for the tenth anniversary?"

"Tin or aluminum," the jeweler answered with a snort. "You won't find either here. But there's a recycling plant just down the river."

Mitch smiled. "I think I'll break with tradition."

"Actually, diamond jewelry is the nontraditional gift for the tenth. And I can show you plenty of that. What would you like to see? I've got bracelets and necklaces and even some watches."

"How about a ring?" Mitch said. "Something different from an engagement ring or a wedding ring. Unique. Like her. Special."

The jeweler smiled. "I think I have just the ring for you." He disappeared into the back room and emerged a few minutes later with a leather case tucked under his arm. Indicating a seat for Mitch, he took his place on the other side of the counter and carefully opened the case. Soft red velvet parted to reveal rows of sparkling diamond rings.

One ring caught Mitch's eye immediately, and before he could point to it, the jeweler picked the ring up and held it out. "I designed this one myself," he explained. "It's a marquise cut, set in this chevron pattern of smaller baguettes. See how the setting sweeps around the marquise? I've always thought this ring deserved someone special. Maybe your wife is just that lady."

"I think she is," Mitch replied, turning the ring to the right and watching it blaze under the lights of the shop. "It's beautiful and exactly what I want. I'll take it. I assume we can worry about the sizing later. I don't have a clue as to her ring size."

The jeweler nodded. "You just bring her in and we'll fit it perfectly to her finger." He took a long breath. "Well, now, that was easy. I wish I had more customers as determined as you. How would you like to pay for this?"

Mitch reached into the deep pocket of his sweatpants and pulled out his wallet. He withdrew the platinum bank card stamped with the name of his father's law firm and snapped it down on the glass case. "This should take care of it," he said with a smile, enjoying the thought of his father's face once the bill arrived. First, five hundred dollars' worth of flowers and now an eight-thousand-dollar ring. Dad would not be happy.

But Mitch considered it payback on the debt the firm owed him. He'd worked his ass off for nine years and didn't have a thing to show for it—except a clear conscience and a definite distaste for his father's business ethics. Every bit of equity he owned in the firm he gave up the day he walked out. He'd consider the money a payment toward his depleted trust fund, a trust fund he'd raided to make up for the firm's mercenary behavior.

He watched the jeweler first place the ring in a red velvet box, then carefully write up the bill of sale. He pushed it across the counter for Mitch to sign, along with the credit card slip. Then after he'd examined both, the old man handed Mitch his card.

"I hope she loves wearing it as much as I loved making it," he said.

"I hope she does, too." Mitch slipped the tiny box in his pocket and turned toward the door, then hesitated. "One more thing, what is your return policy?"

A white eyebrow shot up, and the jeweler gave Mitch a wary look. "You don't think she'll like it?"

He considered the matter for a moment, then frowned. "I'm not sure. I hope she does. But you know women. What if she doesn't?"

The jeweler gave him a smile and waved the credit card form. "I'll just hold on to this for a day. If you don't come back by tomorrow noon, I'll put it through."

Mitch sent him a grateful smile. "Thanks, I'd appreciate that."

The sun had driven away the mist by the time Mitch stepped out of the jewelry shop. He slipped his hand back into his pocket and idly fingered the soft velvet box, turning it over and over in his palm as he walked.

An image of Lianne's face swirled in his mind and invaded his senses, and he allowed himself to linger over it for a long moment. The ring was perfect, a flawless symbol of what she meant to him. Fresh and new and sparkling with possibilities, just like their relationship.

He thought back to the first ring he'd given her, a twenty-thousand-dollar solitaire that his mother had picked out. He hadn't even accompanied her to the jeweler, trusting her to choose a ring that would be appropriate for the wife of a Cooper.

He squeezed the box in his hand. From now on, he'd make his own choices, for his life and for Lianne's. And though he wasn't absolutely sure of what lay ahead, as long as Lianne was by his side, he'd be able to handle anything that came along.

Mitch whistled as he walked the rest of the way back to his apartment. For the first time since this anniversary party had been planned, he was actually looking forward to it.

"I'M JUST SUPPOSED to bring you up here and leave you," Shelly said emphatically. "Those were my instructions."

Lianne looked around the elegant hotel suite. "But I don't understand. There's no one here. Isn't this supposed to be a party? Where is Mrs. Pettigrew and everyone else?"

Shelly cocked her head toward the bed. "There's a note on top of that garment bag. Maybe you should read it."

Lianne slowly walked over to the bed, glancing back at the door when she heard it close. The room was silent except for the muted sound of Boston's late-afternoon rush hour on the street below. Dropping her purse on the bed, she shrugged out of her coat, then draped it across the quilted coverlet. With a hesitant hand, she picked up the cream-colored vellum envelope and opened it.

Inside she found an engraved invitation for the party. "Mitch and Lianne Cooper cordially invite you to celebrate their tenth wedding anniversary with them," she read softly. A party to be held in one of the reception rooms in this very hotel. Her gaze dropped to the bottom of the invitation, to a note written in Eunice's elegant hand. "I knew you'd want a new dress for the occasion. I hope you like it."

Lianne let the invitation flutter to the bed, then reached out for the garment bag and unzipped it. Inside was a romantic ecru-colored gown, Victorian in style, fashioned with layers of flowing embroidery and tiny seed pearls. She drew the dress out of the bag and held it up to her. The hem ended just above her ankles and the neckline revealed just enough to be alluring.

She bit her lip. It looked a lot like a wedding dress to her. Not the typical style of gown, but one similar to the nontraditional gowns she'd seen advertised in *Happily Ever After*. How could she wear this? She wasn't a bride—or even a happily married woman—at least not at the present time.

And what would Mitch think when he saw her in this? He'd probably take it as a sign of total capitulation on her part, an indication that she'd like nothing better than to be his bride again. No, she wasn't going to wear it. She'd stay with the simple yet elegant suit she wore now.

A tiny groan escaped her lips. But what about Mrs. Pettigrew? Eunice had worked so hard to put this anniversary party together, and all for a couple who wasn't even married. The least she could do was make her happy and wear the dress she'd so lovingly chosen. She examined the embroidery a bit more closely to find tiny cabbage roses scattered among the pearls. She smiled.

"All right, Eunice. I'll wear the dress, but all in the name of romance."

It fit perfectly, the slender cut molding to her body as if it had been made just for her. She found shoes, a half size too big, and hose beneath the bag. And a long narrow box that contained a pearl choker and drop earrings that looked vaguely familiar. The cabbage rose clasp reminded her of one that she'd seen Eunice wearing at the office.

She had just snapped the choker in place when a knock sounded on the door. Glancing over her shoulder, she drew a deep breath, then turned to cross the room. Eunice stood outside the door, a wide smile on her flushed face. She was dressed like the mother of the bride, in chiffon with a sheer overlay imprinted with her trademark roses.

"Here you are!" she cried, bustling into the room. "So? How do you like our surprise? Isn't it just the most romantic thing? It was all your husband's idea, but I just couldn't help but get involved. I've become rather fond of your Mitch." She held out her arms, and

Lianne reluctantly stepped forward for a hug. "You look absolutely lovely, my dear. That dress suits you. And your hair is perfect."

Lianne absently reached up to touch a wayward tendril; it had escaped from her upswept hair and brushed her temple. "This really is quite a surprise," she lied. Well, the dress was a surprise even if the party wasn't.

Eunice gave her hand a reassuring pat. "You look a little shell-shocked, my dear. But you had better get a hold of yourself. There are many more wonderful and romantic surprises to come. You know, Mr. Pettigrew and I never had children of our own. Oh, we spoil our nieces and nephews and their children, but it's not the same."

"I'm sorry," Lianne said. "I just assumed all those photos in your office were your children."

"Oh, no. There will be no weddings for me to help plan, no birthday parties for grandchildren to coordinate. That's why I had so much fun planning this party. I've come to think of both of you very fondly. And I hope you'll know that you've given an old romantic lady a treat. And you'll be doing the magazine a great favor. We'll be featuring photos of the party in our November issue."

"What a clever idea!" Lianne cried, forcing a bright smile.

Eunice glanced at her watch. "Well, I'd better let you finish getting ready. The guests should have all arrived and the drinks are probably flowing. Mitch will be up here to fetch you soon. He's been anxious to see you.

My goodness, I don't know how he kept this all a secret, sleeping beside you every night. I was just bursting to tell you!"

With that, Eunice bustled out of the room, giving Lianne a little wave before she closed the door. Feeling a bit numb, Lianne made her way to the bed and slowly sat down to wait for Mitch.

Good grief, this was all happening so fast. She needed a moment to catch her breath. What would she say to him when he showed up? Would she tell him everything that was in her heart, just blurt it out, before he had a chance to speak? Or would she wait until this farce of an anniversary party was over?

She wanted to tell him right away, to get everything out in the open. Her foolish fears had kept them apart too long, and now that she'd decided to admit her love for him, she wanted their life together to start without any delay. She drew a shaky breath.

Lianne knotted her fingers together, willing him to be on the other side of the door, ready now to face him. But when his knock cracked through the silence of the room, she nearly jumped out of her skin.

Another shaky breath and she was on her feet. With a silent prayer, Lianne pulled the door open to find Mitch standing in the hallway, a rueful smile twisting his lips. She opened her mouth to say hello, but her gaze dropped from his face to his clothing.

A giggle burst unbidden from her lips, and she pressed her fingers to her mouth. "What are you wearing?"

Mitch held out his arms and made a swaggering turn

in front of her. He was dressed as a Victorian gentleman, complete with starched collar, swallow-tailed coat and brocade vest. It made him look incredibly masculine, but just a bit overdressed. "Like it? I believe it's supposed to match what you have on, although right about now, I'd feel more comfortable wearing your dress. I look like a goofball."

Lianne reached out and grabbed his arm, then drew him inside. "You do not. You look very...dashing."

"I should be dashing to find a closet to hide in," he insisted. He shoved his finger under his collar and winced. "And this shirt is killing me." He paused suddenly, his gaze meeting hers. "I—I didn't plan for my first words to you to be about my shirt."

She smiled hesitantly. "I guess we've both done a lot of thinking about this moment," she said. "About what we were going to say."

"I'm sorry comes to mind."

"For me, too," she said.

Mitch reached out and took her hand in his, studying her fingers for a long moment. "Annie, I apologize for the way I reacted. I mean, when you refused to marry me again. And I understand, considering how I messed up the first time. But I want you to know that this is not like the first time."

"I know," Lianne said, reaching out to touch his chin. Their eyes met again, and she felt a long, slow flood of warmth seep through her body. Every ounce of love he felt was there, in his eyes, those beautiful blue eyes that had suddenly become a mirror of his soul.

"I'm going to make you happy, Annie. And whether that means marrying you or whether it means staying out of your life, I'm going to do it."

"I don't want you out of my life," she said, reaching out to grasp both his hands. His eyes softened a bit, and she saw hope there. "I love you, Mitch. I was too scared to say it before, but I'm not anymore. I want to be with you and to start over. We can forget about the past, and we can build a future together."

"They're all waiting for us downstairs. I never meant for this to get so out of hand, but Eunice—"

Lianne placed her fingers on his lips. "It's all right. We'll just do our best to get through it."

"There's another thing," Mitch said. "It's about Eunice. I wasn't going to tell you until later, but I think you need to know."

"That you told her about her discriminatory hiring practices? I already know, Mitch, and you did the right thing by telling her."

He smiled, then looked toward the door. "There's something else. Actually, two things, and I don't think you're going to be happy about either one."

Lianne frowned, then shrugged. Well, they might as well get everything out in the open. After all, what could possibly spoil a moment as perfect as this? "Go ahead. Tell me."

"First, Mrs. Pettigrew has a minister downstairs. She decided that it might be nice if we renewed our wedding vows."

Lianne blinked in surprise. "A minister? But what are we supposed to say? I want to marry you again,

Mitch, but not at this very minute. I—thought we'd have more time."

"We can make up our own vows," he said. "Just say what's in your heart and it won't be a lie, Annie. I plan to spend the rest of my life with you, and if today makes that official, then we won't need another wedding ceremony. And if you don't want it to be official, then it won't be."

He drew her into his arms and pressed his lips to her forehead. "When we got married the first time, I had everything to offer you, except the love you really wanted. And now I have nothing to offer you, except that very same love. I don't have a career anymore. I'm not sure what's going to happen in my professional life. But I do know that I intend to make you happier than you ever could have imagined."

"Oh, Mitch." She looked up at him, tears swimming in her eyes. He bent to kiss her, a kiss so gentle and filled with promise that it made her heart ache.

"I have something for you," he murmured, his mouth still touching hers. "I was going to save it for later, but maybe now is the best time."

She drew back. "What is it?"

Lianne watched as he withdrew a tiny box from his vest pocket and held it out to her. She reached for it, but he pulled it away. "You don't have to wear it until you're ready. But I picked it out, just for you. It's something new, a symbol of starting over."

She took the velvet box and slowly opened it. Her eyes went wide at the striking diamond ring inside, a ring so unusual that she had to drag her gaze away to look up at him. "It's incredible. You bought this for me? But how—"

He grinned. "Don't ask how."

"I wasn't going to ask how," she protested. "I was going to say 'But how can I leave a ring as beautiful as this in a box?' I want to wear it, Mitch. Put it on my finger."

Lianne held out her hand, then noticed that she still wore the diamond-studded wedding band.

"What about this?" Mitch asked, twisting it around on her finger.

"Leave it on," she said. "We should save a little something from the past before we start our future. And that will be it. Just a little reminder."

He slipped the ring on her finger and smiled. "It fits perfectly," he said, his voice tinged with amazement. He glanced at her. "Are you as scared as I am?"

"Why are you scared?"

"Because I love you more than I could ever have imagined loving you. I'm thirty-five-years old, Annie, and I'm scared that I might do something to mess up again. I don't want to spend the rest of my life without you. I can't bear the thought of that."

She reached out and touched his cheek, her heart bursting with love for him. "You don't have to be scared, Mitch. This time we're in it together. You and me. Equal partners. Through the best of times and the worst of times, just like the marriage vows say."

Mitch smiled crookedly. "I think that was Dickens who said that. It's 'for better or for worse.'" He stared into her eyes. "I want you to marry me again, Annie. I want a chance to show you how good it can be for us."

She smiled and kissed him gently. "There's a minister downstairs. We could make it real, in our hearts, and take care of the legalities later."

A smile broke across his face. "You mean it? This would be for real, then?"

"I mean it," Lianne replied. "Let's go get married all over again."

With an irrepressible grin, he held out his arm and she slipped her hand through it.

"By the way, what was the other bit of bad news you were going to give me?" she asked.

He stopped, then frowned, and she felt a flutter of fear snake through her. But then his smile returned. "There's a hat that goes with this outfit. A big, ugly top hat. I left it downstairs. That's not going to make you change your mind, is it?"

Lianne laughed, then pushed up on her tiptoes and kissed him squarely on the cheek. "Not a chance. I'm not letting you off the hook so easily this time, Mitch Cooper."

Mitch straightened, then gave her hand a squeeze. "Then, Mrs. Soon-to-be-Cooper-for-the-second-time, let's get going." He gave her a wicked grin. "Because I've got a hell of a honeymoon planned for us."

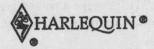

Take 4 bestselling love stories FREE

Plus get a FREE surprise gift!

Special Limited-time Offer

Mail to Harlequin Reader Service®

3010 Walden Avenue
P.O. Box 1867
Buffalo, N.Y. 14240-1867

YES! Please send me 4 free Harlequin Temptation® novels and my free surprise gift. Then send me 4 brand-new novels every month, which I will receive before they appear in bookstores. Bill me at the low price of $2.90 each plus 25¢ delivery and applicable sales tax, if any.* That's the complete price and a savings of over 10% off the cover prices—quite a bargain! I understand that accepting the books and gift places me under no obligation ever to buy any books. I can always return a shipment and cancel at any time. Even if I never buy another book from Harlequin, the 4 free books and the surprise gift are mine to keep forever.

142 BPA A3UP

Name	(PLEASE PRINT)	
Address	Apt. No.	
City	State	Zip

This offer is limited to one order per household and not valid to present Harlequin Temptation® subscribers. *Terms and prices are subject to change without notice. Sales tax applicable in N.Y.

UTEMP-696   ©1990 Harlequin Enterprises Limited

As Seen on TV!

Free Gift Offer

With a Free Gift proof-of-purchase
from any Harlequin® book, you can receive
a beautiful cubic zirconia pendant.

This stunning marquise-shaped stone is a genuine cubic
zirconia—accented by an 18" gold tone necklace.
(Approximate retail value $19.95)

Send for yours today...
compliments of ◆HARLEQUIN®

To receive your free gift, a cubic zirconia pendant, send us one original proof-of-
purchase, photocopies not accepted, from the back of any Harlequin Romance®,
Harlequin Presents®, Harlequin Temptation®, Harlequin Superromance®, Harlequin
Intrigue®, Harlequin American Romance®, or Harlequin Historicals® title available in
February, March or April at your favorite retail outlet, together with the Free Gift
Certificate, plus a check or money order for $1.65 U.S./$2.15 CAN. (do not send cash) to
cover postage and handling, payable to Harlequin Free Gift Offer. We will send you the
specified gift. Allow 6 to 8 weeks for delivery. Offer good until April 30, 1997, or while
quantities last. Offer valid in the U.S. and Canada only.

Free Gift Certificate

Name: _____

Address: _____

City: _____ State/Province: _____ Zip/Postal Code: _____

Mail this certificate, one proof-of-purchase and a check or money order for postage
and handling to: HARLEQUIN FREE GIFT OFFER 1997. In the U.S.: 3010 Walden
Avenue, P.O. Box 9071, Buffalo NY 14269-9057. In Canada: P.O. Box 604, Fort Erie,
Ontario L2Z 5X3.

FREE GIFT OFFER   084-KEZ

ONE PROOF-OF-PURCHASE
To collect your fabulous FREE GIFT, a cubic zirconia pendant, you must include this
original proof-of-purchase for each gift with the properly completed Free Gift Certificate.

084-KEZ

HARLEQUIN®

COMING NEXT MONTH

#629 OUTRAGEOUS Lori Foster
Blaze

One minute, a sexy-as-sin cop is rescuing Emily Cooper from
drunken hoodlums. Five minutes later, he's tearing his clothes off
in front of a group of voracious women. What kind of man is he...
and why can't Emily keep her hands off him? Little does she know
that Judd Sanders really *is* a cop, whose "cover" leaves him a little
too *uncovered* for his liking!

#630 ONE ENCHANTED NIGHT Debra Carroll
It Happened One Night...

Lucy Weston doesn't believe her aunt can conjure up a man from
her dusty book of love spells, but she agrees to help try. Soon after,
there's a knock at the door, and a gorgeous, unconscious man falls
into her arms. Before long the sexy stranger has also fallen into
Lucy's bed. But no one, not even her fantasy lover, knows who
he is....

#631 TWICE THE SPICE Patricia Ryan
Double Dare

Meet shy, studious Emma Sutcliffe and her flamboyant identical
twin, Zara. And see what happens when Emma reluctantly takes on
her sister's identity, her daring clothes and a risky adventure with
the sexiest man she's ever met. And then, next month, don't miss
Harlequin Intrigue #420, *Twice Burned*, for Zara's gripping story.

#632 THE TROUBLE WITH TONYA Lorna Michaels
Tonya Brewster is a walking disaster area. She can't hold a job,
isn't capable of driving within the speed limit and hasn't had a date
in who knows how long! But when she sets her sights on rugged,
hunky Kirk Butler, he doesn't stand a chance. Because Kirk has no
idea just how *much* trouble Tonya can be....

You're About to Become a *Privileged* *Woman*

Reap the rewards of fabulous free gifts and benefits with proofs-of-purchase from Harlequin and Silhouette books

Pages & Privileges™

It's our way of thanking you for buying our books at your favorite retail stores.

PROOF OF PURCHASE HT-PP23
Offer expires March 31, 1997

Pages & Privileges™

Harlequin and Silhouette— the most privileged readers in the world!

For more information about Harlequin and Silhouette's PAGES & PRIVILEGES program call the Pages & Privileges Benefits Desk: 1-503-794-2499

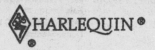

HARLEQUIN ®

HT-PP23